STRANGE UNIVERSE

STRANGE UNIVERSE

AN ANTHOLOGY OF SCIENCE FICTION

CHOSEN BY

AMABEL WILLIAMS-ELLIS & MICHAEL PEARSON

BLACKIE: GLASGOW AND LONDON

Copyright © 1974 Blackie & Son Limited

ISBN 0 216 89714 9

Blackie & Son Limited, Bishopbriggs, Glasgow G64 2NZ
5 Fitzhardinge Street, London, W1H 0DL
Printed in Great Britain by Thomson Litho, East Kilbride, Scotland

CONTENTS

ACKNOWLEDGEMENTS

PUPPET SHOW by Fredric Brown
Reprinted from *The Best of Sci-Fi 4* by permission of John Farquharson Ltd.

THE CONSPIRATORS by James White
Reprinted from *The Aliens Among Us* by permission of E. J. Carnell Literary Agency.

OUCH! by Piers Anthony
Adapted from the first two chapters of *Prostho Plus* by permission of Victor Gollancz Ltd. and E. J. Carnell Literary Agency.

EVIDENCE by Isaac Asimov
Reprinted from *I, Robot* by permission of Dennis Dobson Ltd. and Doubleday and Company Inc.

THE SUBWAYS OF TAZOO by Colin Kapp
Reprinted from *The Best from New Writings* in SF by permission of E. J. Carnell Literary Agency.

THE MACHINE STOPS by E. M. Forster
Reprinted from *Collected Short Stories* by permission of Sidgwick and Jackson Ltd. and Harcourt Brace Jovanovich Inc.

THE AQUATIC UNCLE by Italo Calvino
Reprinted from *Cosmicomics* by permission of Jonathan Cape Ltd. and Hartcourt Brace Jovanovich Inc.

Every effort has been made to trace the ownership of selections included in this anthology in order to secure permission to reprint copyright material and to make full acknowledgement of their use. If any error of omission has occurred, it is purely inadvertent and will be corrected in subsequent editions upon written notification to the publisher, Blackie and Son Ltd., Wester Cleddens Road, Bishopbriggs, Glasgow, G64 2NZ.

PREFACE

Science fiction stories are by their very nature 'out of the ordinary' but we think you will find one piece in this collection that is quite exceptional. It is the tale by E. M. Forster, one of the most eminent of English writers. Forster is much admired for his sensitive and delicate prose style, and style, sadly, is not always a strong point of writers who specialize in Science Fiction.

Four of the stories in this volume will, we hope, amuse you as well as provide food for thought. A sad feature of the current age is that as fast as man gains sophistication in terms of technological knowledge and social awareness, he appears to lose it in terms of humour. Much of what passes as humorous these days is regrettably heavy-handed and dull, and Science Fiction has not escaped this decline. One reason for this is that S.F. follows current attitudes and modes of thought more closely than almost any other type of imaginative writing—probably because of its rapid 'turnover'. The past decade, for example, has seen an increasing interest in the problems of sociology, man-machine communications and sub-atomic physics, and, lately, S.F. has echoed, and occasionally anticipated, these trends. At the same time, however, the contemporary fashion in humour has made its mark, and much supposedly 'amusing' S.F. is nowadays laboured and stilted. So we have included stories such as "Puppet Show" and "The Aquatic Uncle", in which we think the humour is light and skilful. We hope you will agree.

Finally, it is perhaps worth pointing out that S.F. is one of the forms of writing that successfully span the generation gap. For instance, there is a difference in age of nearly half-a-century between your two editors—a fact which we believe helps us in our sampling. Although we have different points of view about many things, one thing that does unite us is a common interest in really high-quality Science Fiction.

AMABEL WILLIAMS-ELLIS
MICHAEL PEARSON

Puppet Show

FREDRIC BROWN

Visitors from Outer Space have featured in many science fiction stories, and they have come in all shapes and sizes. But what will they really be like? And for that matter, how will we recognize them? It might not be all that easy . . .

Horror came to Cherrybell at a little after noon on a blistering hot day in August.

Perhaps that is redundant; *any* August day in Cherrybell, Arizona, is blistering hot. It is on Highway 89, about forty miles south of Tucson and about thirty miles north of the Mexican border. It consists of two filling stations, one on each side of the road to catch travellers going in both directions, a general store, a beer-and-wine-licence-only tavern, a tourist-trap-type trading post for tourists who can't wait until they reach the border to start buying serapes and huaraches, a deserted hamburger stand, and a few 'dobe houses inhabited by Mexican-Americans who work in Nogales, the border town to the south, and who, for God knows what reason, prefer to live in Cherrybell and commute, some of them in Model T Fords. The sign on the highway says, CHERRYBELL, POP. 42, but the sign exaggerates; Pop died last year—Pop Anders, who ran the now deserted hamburger stand—and the correct figure should be 41.

Horror came to Cherrybell mounted on a burro led by an ancient, dirty and grey-bearded desert rat of a prospector who later gave the name of Dade Grant. Horror's name was Garvane. He was approximately nine feet tall but so thin, almost a stick-man, that he could not have weighed over a hundred pounds. Old Dade's donkey—the burro—carried him easily, despite the fact that his feet dragged in the sand on either side. Being dragged through the sand for, as it later turned out, well over five miles hadn't caused the slightest wear on the shoes—more like buskins, they were—which constituted all that he wore except for a pair of what could have been swimming trunks, in robin's-egg blue. But it wasn't his dimensions that made him horrible to look upon; it was his *skin*. It looked red, raw. It looked as though he had been skinned alive, and the skin replaced raw side out. His skull, his face, were equally narrow or elongated; otherwise in every visible way he appeared human—or at least humanoid. Unless you count such little things as the fact that his hair was a robin's-egg blue to match his trunks, as were his eyes and his boots. Blood-red and light blue.

Casey, owner of the tavern, was the first one to see them coming across the plain, from the direction of the mountain range to the east. He'd stepped out of the back door of his tavern for a breath of fresh, if hot, air. They were about one hundred yards away at that time, and already he could see the utter alienness of the figure on the led burro. Just alienness at that distance, the horror came only at closer range. Casey's jaw dropped and stayed down until the strange trio was about fifty yards away, then he started slowly toward them. There are people who run at the sight of the unknown, others who advance to meet it. Casey advanced, slowly, to meet it.

Still in the wide open, twenty yards from the back of the little tavern, he met them. Dade Grant stopped and dropped the rope by which he was leading the burro. The burro stood still and dropped its head. The stick-man stood up simply by planting his feet solidly and standing, astride the burro. He stepped one leg across it and stood a moment, leaning his weight against his hands on the burro's back, and then sat down in the sand. "High gravity planet," he said. "Can't stand long."

"Kin I get water fer my burro?" the prospector asked Casey. "Must be purty thirsty by now. Hadda leave water bags, some other things, so it could carry—" He jerked a thumb toward the red-and-blue horror.

Casey was just realizing that it *was* a horror. At a distance the colour combination seemed only mildly hideous, but close up—the skin was rough and seemed to have veins on the outside and looked moist (although it wasn't) and *damn* if it didn't look just like he had his skin peeled off and put back on inside out. Or just peeled off, period. Casey had never seen anything like it and hoped he wouldn't ever see anything like it again.

Casey felt something behind him and looked over his shoulder. Others had seen now and were coming, but the nearest of them, a pair of boys, were ten yards behind him *"Muchachos,"* he called out. *"Agua por el burro. Pronto."*

He looked back and said, "What—? Who—?"

"Name's Dade Grant," said the prospector, putting out a hand, which Casey took absently. When he let go of it it jerked back over the desert rat's shoulder, thumb indicating the thing that sat on the sand. *"His* name's Garvane, he tells me. He's an extra something or other, and he's some kind of minister."

Casey nodded at the stick-man and was glad to get a nod in return instead of an extended hand. "I'm Manuel Casey," he said. "What does he mean, an extra something?"

The stick-man's voice was unexpectedly deep and vibrant. "I am an extraterrestrial. And a minister plenipotentiary."

Surprisingly, Casey was a moderately well-educated man and knew both of those phrases; he was probably the only person in Cherrybell who would have known the second one. Less surprisingly, considering the speaker's appearance, he believed both of them.

"What can I do for you, sir?" he asked. "But first, why not come in out of the sun?"

"No, thank you. It's a bit cooler here than they told me it would be, but I'm quite comfortable. This is equivalent to a cool spring evening on my planet. And as to what you can do for me, you can notify your authorities of my presence. I believe they will be interested."

Well, Casey thought, by blind luck he's hit the best man for his purpose within at least twenty miles. Manuel Casey was half Irish, half Mexican. He had a half-brother who was half Irish and half assorted-American, and the half-brother was a bird colonel at Davis-Monthan Air Force Base in Tucson.

He said, "Just a minute, Mr Garvane, I'll telephone. You, Mr Grant, would you want to come inside?"

"Naw, I don't mind sun. Out in it all day ever' day. An' Garvane here, he ast me if I'd stick with him till he was finished with what he's gotta do here. Said he'd gimme somethin' purty vallable. Somethin' 'lectronic—"

"An electronic battery-operated portable ore indicator," Garvane said. "A simple little device, indicates presence of a concentration of ore up to two miles, indicates kind, grade, quantity and depth."

Casey gulped, excused himself, and pushed through the gathering crowd into his tavern. He had Colonel Casey on the phone in one minute, but it took another four minutes to convince him that he was neither drunk nor joking.

Twenty-five minutes after that there was a noise in the sky, a noise that swelled and then died as a four-man helicopter sat down and shut off its rotors a dozen yards from an extraterrestrial, two men and a burro. Casey alone had had the courage to rejoin the trio from the desert; there were other spectators, but they still held well back.

Colonel Casey, a major, a captain and a lieutenant who was the helicopter's pilot all came out and ran over. The stick-man stood up, all nine feet of him; from the effort it cost him to stand you could tell that he was used to a much lighter gravity than Earth's. He bowed, repeated his name and the identification of himself as an extraterrestrial and a minister plenipotentiary. Then he apologized for sitting down again, explained why it was necessary, and sat down.

The colonel introduced himself and the three who had come with him. "And now, sir, what can we do for you?"

The stick-man made a grimace that was probably intended as a smile. His teeth were the same light blue as his hair and eyes.

"You have a cliché, 'Take me to your leader.' I do not ask that. In fact, I *must* remain here. Nor do I ask that any of your leaders be brought here. That would be impolite. I am perfectly willing for you to represent them, to talk to you and let you question me. But I do ask one thing.

"You have tape recorders. I ask that before I talk or answer questions you have one brought. I want to be sure that the message your leaders eventually receive is full and accurate."

"Fine," the colonel said. He turned to the pilot. "Lieutenant, get on the radio in the whirlybird and tell them to get us a tape recorder faster than possible. It can be dropped by para— No, that'd take longer, rigging it for a drop. Have them send it by another helicopter." The lieutenant turned to go. "Hey," the colonel said. "Also fifty yards of extension cord. We'll have to plug it in inside Manny's tavern."

The lieutenant sprinted for the helicopter.

The others sat and sweated a moment and then Manuel Casey stood up. "That's a half-hour wait," he said, "and if we're going to sit here in the sun, who's for a bottle of cold beer? You, Mr Garvane?"

"It is a cold beverage, is it not? I am a bit chilly. If you have something hot—?"

"Coffee, coming up. Can I bring you a blanket?"

"No, thank you. It will not be necessary."

Casey left and shortly returned with a tray with half-a-dozen bottles of cold beer and a cup of steaming coffee. The lieutenant was back by then. Casey put the tray down and served the stick-man first, who sipped the coffee and said, "It is delicious."

Colonel Casey cleared his throat. "Serve our prospector friend next, Manny. As for us—well, drinking is forbidden on duty, but it was 112 in the shade in Tucson, and this is hotter and also is *not* in the shade. Gentlemen, consider yourselves on official leave for as long as it takes you to drink one bottle of beer, or until the tape recorder arrives, whichever comes first."

The beer was finished first, but by the time the last of it had vanished, the second helicopter was within sight and sound. Casey asked the stick-man if he wanted more coffee. The offer was politely declined. Casey looked at Dade Grant and winked and the desert rat winked back, so Casey went in for two more bottles, one apiece for the Civilian terrestrials. Coming back he met the lieutenant arriving with the extension cord and returned as far as the doorway to show him where to plug it in.

When he came back, he saw that the second helicopter had brought its full complement of four, besides the tape recorder. There were, besides the pilot who had flown it, a technical sergeant who was skilled in its operation and who was now making adjustments on it, and a lieutenant-colonel and a warrant officer who had come along for the ride or because they had been made curious by the request for a tape recorder to be rushed to Cherrybell, Arizona, by air. They were standing gaping at the stick-man and whispered conversations were going on.

The colonel said, "Attention," quietly, but it brought complete silence. "Please sit down, gentlemen. In a rough circle. Sergeant, if you rig your mike in the centre of the circle, will it pick up clearly what any one of us may say?"

"Yes, sir. I'm almost ready."

Ten men and one extraterrestrial humanoid sat in a rough circle, with the microphone hanging from a small tripod in the approximate centre. The humans were sweating profusely; the humanoid shivered slightly. Just outside the circle, the burro stood dejectedly, its head low. Edging closer, but still about five yards away, spread out now in a semicircle, was the entire population of Cherrybell who had been at home at the time; the stores and the filling stations were deserted.

The technical sergeant pushed a button and the tape recorder's reel started to turn. "Testing... testing," he said. He held down the rewind button for a second and then pushed the playback button. "Testing... testing," said the recorder's speaker. Loud and clear. The sergeant pushed the rewind button, then the erase one to clear the tape. Then the stop button.

"When I push the next button, sir," he said to the colonel, "we'll be recording."

The colonel looked at the tall extraterrestrial, who nodded, and then the colonel nodded at the sergeant. The sergeant pushed the recording button.

"My name is Garvane," said the stick-man, slowly and clearly. "I am from a planet of a star which is not listed in your star catalogues, although the global cluster in which it is one of 90,000 stars is known to you. It is, from here, in the direction of the centre of the galaxy, at a distance of over four thousand light-years.

"However, I am not here as a representative of my planet or my people, but as minister plenipotentiary of the Galactic Union, a federation of the enlightened civilizations of the galaxy, for the good of all. It is my assignment to visit you and decide, here and now, whether or not you are to be welcomed to join our federation.

"You may now ask questions freely. However, I reserve the right to postpone answering some of them until my decision has been made. If the decision is favorable, I will then answer all questions, including the ones I have postponed answering meanwhile. Is that satisfactory?"

"Yes," said the colonel. "How did you come here? A spaceship?"

"Correct. It is overhead right now, in orbit twenty-two thousand miles out, so it revolves with the earth and stays over this one spot. I am under observation from it, which is one reason I prefer to remain here in the open. I am to signal it when I want it to come down to pick me up."

"How do you know our language? Are you telepathic?"

"No, I am not. And nowhere in the galaxy is any race telepathic except among its own members. I was taught your language for this purpose. We have had observers among you for many centuries—by *we*, I mean the Galactic Union, of course. Quite obviously, I could not pass as an Earthman, but there are other races who can. Incidentally, they are not spies, or agents; they have in no way tried to affect you; they are observers and that is all."

"What benefits do we get from joining your union, if we are asked and if we accept?" the colonel asked.

"First, a quick course in the fundamental social sciences which will end your tendency to fight among yourselves and end or at least control your aggressions. After we are satisfied that you have accomplished that and it is safe for you to do so, you will be given space travel, and many other things, as rapidly as you are able to assimilate them."

"And if we are not asked, or refuse?"

"Nothing. You will be left alone; even our observers will be withdrawn. You will work out your own fate—either you will render your planet uninhabited and uninhabitable within the next century, or you will master social science yourselves and again be candidates for membership and again be offered membership. We will check from time to time and if and when it appears certain that you are not going to destroy yourselves, you will again be approached."

"Why the hurry, now that you're here? Why can't you stay long enough for our leaders, as you call them, to talk to you in person?"

"Postponed. The reason is not important but it is complicated, and I simply do not wish to waste time explaining."

"Assuming your decision is favourable, how will we get in touch with you to let you know *our* decision? You know enough about us, obviously, to know that *I* can't make it."

"We will know your decision through our observers. One condition of acceptance is full and uncensored publication in your newspapers of this interview, verbatim from the tape we are now using to record it. Also of all deliberations and decisions of your government."

"And other governments? We can't decide unilaterally for the world."

"Your government has been chosen for a start. If you accept, we shall furnish the techniques that will cause the others to fall in line quickly—and those techniques do not involve force or the threat of force."

"They must be *some* techniques," said the colonel wryly, "if they'll make one certain country I don't have to name fall into line without even a threat."

"Sometimes the offer of reward is more significant than the use of a threat. Do you think the country you do not wish to name would like your country colonizing planets of far stars before they even reach the moon? But that is a minor point, relatively. You may trust the techniques."

"It sounds almost too good to be true. But you said that you are to decide, here and now, whether or not we are to be invited to join. May I ask on what factors you will base your decision?"

"One is that I am—was, since I already have—to check your degree of xenophobia. In the loose sense in which you use it, that means fear of strangers. We have a word that has no counterpart in your vocabulary: it means fear of and revulsion toward *aliens*. I—or at least a member of my race—was chosen to make the first overt contact with you. Because I am what you would call roughly humanoid—as you are what I would call roughly humanoid—I am probably more horrible, more repulsive, to you than many completely different species would be. Because to you I am a caricature of a human being, I am more horrible to you than a being who bears no remote resemblance to you.

"You may think you *do* feel horror at me, and revulsion, but believe me, you have passed that test. There *are* races in the galaxy who can never be members of the federation, no matter how they advance otherwise, because they are violently and incurably xenophobic; they could never face or talk to an alien of any species. They would either run screaming from him or try to kill him instantly. From watching you and these people"—he waved a long arm at the civilian population of Cherrybell not far outside the circle of the conference—"I know you feel revulsion at the sight of me, but believe me, it is relatively slight and certainly curable. You have passed that test satisfactorily."

"And are there other tests?"

"One other. But I think it is time that I—" Instead of finishing the sentence, the stick-man lay back flat on the sand and closed his eyes.

The colonel started to his feet. "What in *hell*?" he said. He walked quickly around the mike's tripod and bent over the recumbent extraterrestrial, putting an ear to the bloody-appearing chest.

As he raised his head, Dade Grant, the grizzled prospector, chuckled. "No heartbeat, Colonel, because no heart. But I may leave him as a souvenir for you and you'll find much more interesting things inside him than heart and guts. Yes, he is a puppet whom I have been operating, as your Edgar Bergen operates his—what's his name?—oh yes, Charlie McCarthy. Now that he has served his purpose, he is deactivated. You can go back to your place, Colonel."

Dade Grant was peeling off his beard and wig. He

rubbed a cloth across his face to remove make-up and was revealed as a handsome young man. He said, "What he told you, or what you were told through him, was true as far as it went. He is only a simulacrum, yes, but he is an exact duplicate of a member of one of the intelligent races of the galaxy, the one toward whom you would be disposed—if you were violently and incurably xenophobic—to be most horrified by, according to our psychologists. But we did not bring a real member of his species to make first contact because they have a phobia of their own, agoraphobia—fear of space. They are highly civilized and members in good standing of the federation, but they never leave their own planet. Our observers assure us you don't have *that* phobia. But they were unable to judge in advance the degree of your xenophobia, and the only way to test it was to bring along something in lieu of someone to test it against, presumably to let him make the initial contact."

The colonel sighed audibly. "I can't say this doesn't relieve me in one way. We could get along with humanoids, yes, and we will when we have to. But I'll admit it's a relief to learn that the master race of the galaxy is, after all, human instead of only humanoid. And the second test?"

"You are undergoing it now. Call me—" He snapped his fingers. "What's the name of Bergen's second-string puppet, after Charlie McCarthy?"

The colonel hesitated, but the tech sergeant supplied the answer. "Mortimer Snerd."

"Right. So call me Mortimer Snerd, and now I think it is time that I—" He lay back flat on the sand and closed his eyes just as the stick-man had done a few minutes before.

The burro raised its head and put it into the circle over the shoulder of the tech sergeant.

"That takes care of the puppets, Colonel," it said. "And now, what's this bit about it being important that the master race be human or at least humanoid? What is a master race?"

The Conspirators

JAMES WHITE

A cat, a canary called Singer, and sundry mice and guinea pigs are the 'heroes' of this cautionary tale. Experimental animals in a space probe, they are to be used for scientific purposes on newly discovered planets. Or are they?

Something had gone wrong. It was outside his range, but Felix caught a sharp, incoherent sensation of mingled shock, loss, and panic in the instant that it happened. He floated, outwardly unconcerned, in the middle of the corridor which led to the Biology Section, and waited for the details to come down the line.

A few minutes later the relay who was clinging to the wallnet at the end of the corridor began sending him the facts. The news was very bad.

It seemed that the Small One whose job it was to damage certain tiny but important circuits in the Communications Room for purposes connected with the Escape had had an accident. Singer had seen it happen—Felix had guessed it was Singer. Even on the fourth leg of a relay the thought pattern was unmistakable; all emotion and not enough fact—the Small One had jumped for cover when he heard the crewman coming, misjudged, and landed on a live section. It was only a couple of hundred volts, but that was an awful lot to a Small One—he was very thoroughly dead. What was left of him was floating in plain sight, and Singer was rapidly killing himself with his frenzied attempts at holding the crewman's attention, because if the man noticed the body, and the disconnected wiring beside it, he might be suspicious. Singer wanted somebody to do something, *quick*. The message ended with a sense-free garble of fear, urgency, and panic that was almost hysteria.

To another Small One concealed in a ventilator at the

other end of the corridor, Felix relayed the message exactly as he'd received it. But he had an addition to make. He sent, "Include this. Felix to Whitey. I think I can handle this. Send someone to replace me—I'm on relay duty half way along corridor Five-C—I'm going to Communications." He wriggled furiously until he made contact with the wall-net, then launched himself down the corridor towards the intersection leading to the scene of the accident.

Usually Felix left important decisions to the Small Ones. They had the brains. He didn't know why he'd taken the initiative this time. Whitey, he thought, might not be pleased.

He was able to enter the Communications Room and get to the Small One's body without the crewman seeing him. Singer, though impractical in many ways, could create quite a diversion when he wanted to. Singer was fluttering around the man's head in tight circles, and the man was making ineffectual grabs at him and wondering loudly what had got into the blasted thing. He had eyes and thoughts, Felix knew, only for Singer. Good.

The fur on the body was badly scorched, and Felix's nose told him that parts of the underlying flesh were cooked, too. Suddenly a raw, animal hunger stirred inside him and began to grow, but he fought it down. Since the Change had begun, satisfaction of that nature was not for him. Felix batted the tiny corpse towards the opposite corner of the room, well away from those all-important circuits, then launched himself after it.

When he'd retrieved it and had it settled between his paws, he told Singer, "All right, Bird-brain. You can relax. Better leave now—you're suppose to be afraid of me."

A bright yellow streak of motion, Singer flew out the door and down the corridor. Before he was out of range he returned, "I *am* afraid of you . . . You . . . *savage!*"

Seconds later the crewman caught sight of Felix. Pleased, he said, "Felix! Where've you been hiding yourself?" He grabbed Felix by the neck with one hand and pulled himself into a seat with the other. Clipping in and settling Felix on his lap, he went on, "So you caught a mouse, eh, Felix? But what have you been doing with it? Having a barbecue or something?" He stopped talking then, but his mind was busy. He began to stroke the back of Felix's neck.

Felix didn't feel at all like purring, but he knew that it was expected of him. After a while he began to enjoy it in spite of himself, but that didn't stop him from reading the crewman's thoughts.

A sharp, clear thought—characteristic of the Small Ones—brought him abruptly to full attention. Felix couldn't see the other, but he knew that the Small One was within thirty feet of him—that was the maximum effective range of their telepathy—probably in the emergency spacesuit hanging outside the door that Felix had noticed coming in. The thought said, "Felix, your replacement is in position. Whitey wants you to report."

"Right. Relay this. Felix to Whitey . . ."

For a moment Felix felt awed as he thought of Whitey in Bio-Lab Three—more than half the length of the great Ship away—surrounded by Big Ones, and the Small Ones who weren't on relay duties, and all of them working on the Escape. And of the other telepathic relays that linked Lab Three with places like Seed Storage, Central Control, and Engines. . . . Catching an impatient thought from the Small One out in the corridor, Felix hastily brought his mind back to the report.

". . . This Human is not suspicious," he sent. "The Small One was so badly scorched that the Lab markings have been obliterated, and he thinks it is a Wild One from Seed Storage section. He thinks that I have knocked it against some live wires while playing with it, and that I'm very lucky I didn't meet the same fate myself—there's that old 'nine lives' concept again—but he is wondering why I didn't eat the thing . . ."

Felix knew that a feeling of shocked revulsion was left in the wake of his message as it went down the line. Felix did not share the deep sorrow that the accident had caused among the more intelligent and highly-sensitive Small Ones. He took a perverse pleasure in shocking them sometimes. Without meaning to they made him feel inferior, envious. Felix wasn't proud of these feelings, but there wasn't much he could do about them. The Change was very slow in him.

"... He is not interested in checking any of the room's equipment," Felix continued, "but is impatient to rejoin the bulk of the crew who are packed into Astronomy section all trying to get a closer view of the new planet. He is feeling rebellious at having to stand watch here at a time like this, and is wondering sarcastically if the Captain is expecting the natives—if any—of the planet below to just ring him up.

"At the back of his mind he is feeling angry because the scoutship is unable to make a landing. But neither he nor anyone else suspect that we were responsible for damaging its Planetary Drive coils. The fact that the replacements are also missing they blame on a clerical error in storing or checking the equipment back home. They don't know we've hidden them."

The Human stopped his stroking of Felix and pushed him gently off his lap. Felix ended, "He intends trying to sleep now. Nobody will be coming here, he knows, and he's a light sleeper anyway." He waited a little anxiously for Whitey's reply.

"You've done well, Felix."

Even though coloured by the personalities of nearly a score of the relay entities, the thought was still warm, congratulatory. Then it changed subtly. "Come to the Lab at once, Felix. There is a transport problem."

"Right," Felix answered. "But before I go; the Human is asleep now. If you send somebody to arrange those disconnected wires so's they'll pass visual inspection, nothing can go wrong here."

He intercepted the reply when he was already half way to the Lab. He'd been hurrying. It was:

"Thanks Felix. It is already being done."

When he reached the Lab two of the Big Ones had the ventilator grill moved aside for him. The door was never used for the reason that the Humans kept it fastened, so that opening it would have aroused their suspicions. Felix wriggled through. As he kicked himself across the small anteroom leading into the Lab proper he heard the Big Ones sliding the grill back into position. *Nothing*—especially now that they were so near to success—must be allowed to make the crewmen suspect anything wrong. Even the Big Ones, who weren't too bright, understood that.

Felix hadn't been 'reaching' with his mind—too much telepathy was still inclined to tire him—so he had no warning of what to expect. Weightless, unable to stop himself, he sailed gracefully into the Lab—right smack into the middle of it.

He was hit five times and sent spinning, his nicely timed dive ruined, by flying Big Ones. And he lost track of how often young Small Ones rammed him. Everybody in the place—*and* their young, too, if any—were in rapid motion, sailing from wall to wall, floor to ceiling, and even corner to corner. It looked like a furry snowstorm. When he succeeded at last in reaching a wall-net, he directed a thought at the white mouse clinging to the fur of a Big One on the other side of the room. The thought was wordless, incoherent, an all-embracing question mark.

"They're practising for the evacuation, Felix," Whitey explained. "And that is the problem I mentioned. Some of them—the young, especially—won't be able to make it." Whitey stopped to give instructions to a Big One who was floundering helplessly out in the middle of the Lab. He resumed, "Come over here, Felix. We can 'talk' better at short range."

Felix was again hit several times on the way across by flying Big Ones. But being in collision with a guinea-pig wasn't painful, merely disconcerting, and he hadn't enough dignity left for that to be hurt. He had just settled beside the Big One bearing Whitey when Singer flew in and joined them. The canary hung, wings folded and turning slowly in the draft from the air-conditioning, just six inches from Felix's nose. Felix wondered suddenly what it would be like to bite his head off.

Radiating shock and panic, Singer flapped desperately out of range. "Stop that, Felix!"

Whitey was really angry at him, with the helpless,

frustrated anger that is inspired by the constant misbehaviour of a backward child. Ashamed, Felix addressed Singer.

"Sorry, I didn't mean that. I wouldn't hurt you for anything. Come on back."

Singer fluttered back, nervously, thinking about horrid, insensitive brutes, and great hairy cannibals. He wasn't completely reassured.

Whitey, his anger gone as quickly as it had come, began to state the problem.

"You two know that we intend to evacuate everyone, and you also know how we're going to leave the Ship—in one of the radio-controlled testing rockets. But we've misjudged badly. The distance from the Lab here to the launching slips is a little over five hundred feet, and now we find that there won't be enough time to get everybody to the rocket.

"You see, several trips will have to be made for the young, and the Big Ones are slow and awkward. They've never had the chance to practise long-distance weightless travel like us, and they're very much worse at it than we'd expected. And they're so slow to learn, some of them . . ."

So slow to learn, Felix thought sadly. Just like me. He knew that all three of them were thinking about the Change, and how it had affected them personally, as well as the way it affected their species as a whole.

Not one of them knew for sure just why the Change had come about, but there were theories. The generally accepted one was that the prolonged absence of gravity occasioned by the operation of the Ship's overdrive, or the freedom from their home planet's gravitation, or the removal of some hypothetical radiation given off by the home sun, either singly or taken together had caused a change in the cell structure of the small, relatively simple brains of the animals aboard the Ship. Its result was a steady increase in their I.Q.

The Change, however, did not occur at a uniform rate, but varied with the size of the brain concerned. The small-brained mice were affected first. They developed a high intelligence quickly, and with it the faculty for communicating telepathically. And, as well as reading each other's thoughts, they were able to tap the mind of the crewman who came to the Lab at weekly intervals to replenish the automatic food dispenser which kept them fed.

They learned a lot from him; his duties, his background, what he thought about the other members of the crew, and, most important, the purpose of the Expedition. Also, because he vocalised his thoughts, they learned the language. This increased their understanding of their environment, but it also caused them to make an important assumption based, though they didn't know it, on too little data.

Because the Ship had only been gone from Earth barely four months, and the awful boredom had not yet set in, this particular Human was full to bursting with the glorious thoughts of this first exploration among the stars, the possible colonisation of newly discovered planets, and a warm, brotherly feeling towards everybody in general. And he was naturally kind to animals. He was also the only Human whose mind was available to the animals for reading—no other crewman came within the thirty-foot radius of the Small Ones' telepathy. Their assumption, therefore, was justified.

For six weeks the community of Small Ones existed in the Lab, with servo-mechanisms attending to their every need, happy, contented, and very excited.

They thought they were the Ship's colonists.

Then one day Singer had been put in the Lab. Singer was a completely new species to the Small Ones. He was bright yellow in colour, had 'wings' which made it easy for him to move about in the weightless condition of the Ship, and he produced audible vibrations which were very pleasant to hear. Though he wasn't as bright as the Small Ones, the Change had made him telepathic. He had a lot more information to impart about the Ship and its crew, information that left the Small Ones shocked and horrified. He was able to tell them of their true status aboard the Ship, and of the fate that experimental animals could expect when the time came to test the atmosphere, plant-life, and bacteria of a new planet. Singer also told of a ferocious black monster the Humans called 'Felix' that roamed the Ship, and how the Humans had put him in here to keep the beast from killing him.

Living was suddenly a grim business. They would try to escape, of course, but the Small Ones knew enough about the operation of the ship now to realise how small was the opportunity of doing that. And they couldn't leave the Lab even, because of this thing called Felix. If that had been possible they might have been able to create an opportunity for escape, by sabotage or some other means. But the only thing they could do was wait, and hope that the Big Ones, who also lived in the Lab, would be able to take care of 'Felix' when they became further advanced.

But the Big Ones had been slow, Felix knew, and their bigness was only relative. Luckily they never had to try taking care of him; a scrap between a guinea-pig—or even several guinea-pigs—and a full-grown cat would have been no contest at all.

Felix had been nosing about outside the Lab one day, hoping to catch himself some food 'on the hoof', when he suddenly realized that the animals inside were 'talking' to him. The reason for the strange ability he'd noticed in himself in being able to understand the Humans—even when they didn't speak aloud—was explained to him, and very soon he had more important things on his mind than a craving to eat Small Ones. All at once he had become an important person, an *invaluable* person. The way the Small Ones explained it, his wider knowledge of the Ship and its crew, together with his aid in guiding them to certain key spots, would make an escape not only possible, but highly probable . . .

"Pay attention, Felix!" Whitey radiated sharply. Felix came hastily out of his day-dream, conscious that if he'd been a Human, his face would have been very red.

"I was saying that the Big Ones are slow," Whitey went on, "and awkward. That's partly because we haven't allowed them outside the Lab much; they'd be spotted too easily. But that's the problem now, moving them quickly.

"At the moment I can see no solution. But you two being 'pets', and having the freedom of the Ship, might be able to suggest something." Whitey paused, and the ghastly wordless images they all knew so well surged up from the back of his mind. Experimentation, vivisection, *murder*. Grimly, he went on, "I don't want to leave anybody behind, to *that—*"

He broke off as two reports came, almost simultaneously, from opposite ends of the great Ship.

"Relay from Secondary Engines. Quarter G deceleration has been ordered for three minutes."

"Relay from Control-room. Captain has ordered quarter G deceleration . . . " It was practically a duet.

The telepathic link-ups that ran from all the key points on the Ship to the Lab were fast, efficient, and accurate. But they were just a little slower than the Ship's intercom system. Some of the animals were able to act on the information before the deceleration hit them, and hang on. The rest dropped, an uneven, struggling layer of grey and brown on to the forward wall.

Felix landed the way he always did, crouching, and on his feet. Unfortunately he also landed on a group of eight very young Small Ones. The resultant blast of fear and raw, uninhibited anger from their under-developed minds nearly curdled his brains before he was able to reel off. Then he had to counter the bolts of the outraged parent concerned, even though the adult Small One was intelligent enough to realise that none of it was Felix's fault. There were some things that didn't depend on intelligence, Felix realised, and mother love was one of them.

Abruptly Felix felt awed at himself. He was the muscle man around here—he'd never had thoughts like *that* before. But the feeling left him just as quickly.

While the deceleration lasted Felix listened to the ranting of the Small One, and tried to keep the amusement he felt from showing too much in his mind. He hadn't hurt the youngsters, of course, just frightened them. They were extraordinarily strong for their size, and they were so light that they could take a knocking about that would probably kill Felix. He began to wonder about their toughness, and about the evacuation problem. Suppose . . .

The Small One caught his half-formed thought and radiated a horrified negative. Felix tried to reassure her, but just then weightlessness returned and he launched himself towards Whitey again.

While Felix was still airborne Whitey sent, "I heard some of that, too, Felix. Would you expand on that thought about ferrying the young to the rocket?"

Felix took the mental equivalent of a deep breath. He was acutely conscious of the fact that his thinking, when compared with that of the Small Ones, was slow and almost incoherent at times. But he did his best.

"It is this. I suggest we ferry the young to the launching slips *before* the adults go, instead of at the same time. That way the Big Ones would have only one trip to make, and no matter how inexperienced they were, there would be plenty of time for the journey. With Singer here to help me as look-out, I can transfer them six or eight at a time to the test rocket. And even if a crewman should see me—"

Whitey interrupted: "*How* are you going to move them, Felix?" Every mind in the room was giving him full attention now.

"By pretending to play with them," Felix answered. Hesitantly, he began to explain. "In the old days, before I knew all about the Change, the crew used to give me things to play with. It was great fun . . ." He stopped suddenly, feeling ashamed and embarrassed at the confession he'd just made. Hastily, he went on, "That was before I met you, of course.

"But what I want to say is that I know where some of those playthings are. They are soft, spherical, and their fabric is easily opened. the young ones can hide inside them while I push the things along.

"The Humans won't be suspicious of a cat playing with an old rag ball."

Almost before he had completed his thought the objections were coming thick and fast. Felix found it a little frightening; he had never had so many minds thinking at

him all at once before like this. But somehow, after the first
few minutes, it didn't scare him any more. It was a strange
feeling. He still felt awed by their vastly greater
intelligence, but not as much as before. Now he respected
them—and almost *liked* them—as equals. Possibly it was
the nature of the thoughts they were thinking that brought
about the change in him. Felix could understand their
feelings, but those thoughts hurt.

Impatiently, he interrupted the constant stream of
protest. They were beginning to repeat themselves.

"Whitey! Tell them I'm not going to *eat* the things . . ."

They didn't believe him.

Oh, the Small Ones knew that he meant what he said,
Felix realized, but they didn't trust his—impulses. The less
intelligent Big Ones still thought of him as a semi-
domesticated carnivore, and wouldn't trust him with their
young farther than they could see him. But, he knew if he
could convince the Small Ones that his plan would work,
they could win over the Big Ones.

Whitey hadn't taken sides in the argument yet, so that
left it up to himself. He signalled sharply for attention and
felt pleasantly surprised when he got it at once. He began
his sales-talk.

"This is the position as I see it at the moment," he sent.
"The Ship is in the process of taking up an eight-hour orbit
around the first apparently habitable planet to be
discovered. The planet, not yet named, is referred to by the
crew as Epsilon Aurigae VII and they are very excited
about finding it during the first seven months of their three-
year exploratory voyage.

"From our telepathic relay lines to the Ship's control
centres we know that this orbiting manoeuvre will be
complete in just under three hours, after which most of the
crew will be engaged in mapping the planetary surface,
studying its weather, or just looking at it through
telescopes. Roughly an hour after the Ship takes up its
orbit, two of the big testing rockets will be sent down under
remote control to the surface, for the purpose of collecting
samples of air, soil and liquid from as many widely
separate points on the planet as possible. These rockets will

be guided automatically, and if everything goes off according to plan, we will be on one of them."

Felix paused. He was thinking about the Small One who had died so recently in the Communications Room.

"We have been able," he went on, "to fix the alarm circuits here on the Ship so that the rocket containing us will apparently behave normally, though actually it will be disabled by us at the first suitable landing point so that we can disembark. But we have only one hour—less than an hour, to allow for slip-ups—when the crew will be too busy to notice our movements; and during this period all the animals must be got aboard the test rocket. That means that everyone here, all the Small Ones in Seed Storage, and all the relays scattered about the Ship will have to reach the launching slip and find their places aboard in that short time. And most of them will have to make several trips back and forwards for their young, or . . ." Felix regarded the untrained and clumsy Big Ones " . . . the people who haven't been able to practise weightless travel."

"Whitey says that this is impossible."

The Small Ones knew all this, Felix thought, and the Big Ones should know it, too. But everybody had developed the habit of explaining things several times to the Big Ones—they weren't very bright yet . . . Felix got control of himself quickly. That last thought had been tactless. He hoped the Big Ones had been too busy with their own thoughts to notice his slip.

"Now my idea is that we evacuate the young of both species first, and before the orbiting manoeuvre is completed. That way even the clumsiest—" Felix would have liked to use a kinder word, but it was impossible to lie with the mind "—Big Ones will be able to make their way to the slip in the hour remaining before the test rocket leaves. Also, with everybody making just one trip, the risk of discovery by a crewman will be practically nil. I think I can handle it, but I'll need a lot of help."

Felix was trying to give them the idea that he'd be under their observation all the time, and that even if he had wanted to, he couldn't pull anything. It was the only way, he knew, to get them to agree to his plan.

"There will have to be Small Ones at both ends of the line to load and unload the young, and I'll need Singer to create a diversion should a crewman wander by and want to play with me. And I'll need help with other things, too . . ."

Abruptly he wondered why he was taking all this trouble for them. A short time ago he wouldn't have bothered. What was happening to him?

He ended simply, "I don't see any other way of doing it in time."

Later, as he was propelling a lumpy, brightly-coloured ball filled with eight struggling baby guinea-pigs along the corridor towards the rocket, Felix thought how close it had been. When Whitey agreed to his plan Felix had thought everything would be settled—after all, he was their leader. But it hadn't been like that. There had almost been a civil war before they finally agreed to his plan, and they had wasted more than half an hour with their arguing. They just didn't trust Felix, it seemed.

At the intersection leading to the launching slip Felix let his load collide with the wall-net, landing partly on top of it to keep the springy mesh from bouncing it back again. His passengers immediately shrieked that they were being murdered and they wanted their mothers. Luckily, Felix thought, it was on the telepathic frequency; had it been audible, men would have come running from all over the Ship. Hastily he reassured the Small One on relay duty in the corridor who was radiating anxiety like a fluorescent light tube. At the other end of the corridor he saw Singer fluttering around in a slow loop. That was the all-clear signal. Felix settled his burden solidly between his fore-paws and chest and kicked himself off again.

He couldn't really blame them for not trusting him, he thought, as the corridor walls drifted slowly past. There was still quite a lot of the savage in him. Much of it was due to the slowness of his Change, but a lot was due also to the crewmen who had brought him aboard as the Ship's mascot. They were the non-specialists on the Ship. They did most of the donkey work, and they were, to put it mildly, decidedly uncouth. From their minds Felix had learned practically everything he knew until the time of his meeting with the Small Ones. The result was that he was inclined to think and act like his erstwhile 'masters'. The idiom he used when trying to express his thoughts, and his general air of tough cynicism, made it difficult for the others to trust him completely. It was very hard to convince them that his ideas had changed.

Still, even though he wasn't a nice character, the Small Ones were lucky to have him. They were intelligent, Felix knew; the most intelligent and highly-civilized beings on the Ship—and that included the crew. If they'd only had hands, and a more practical approach to solving their problems, they could have taken over the running of the Ship themselves months ago, and got rid of the Humans. But they weren't tough enough, or practical. When there was any time to spare they used their high intelligence to get into philosophical discussions among themselves, and they were, Felix thought pityingly, terribly unrealistic—soft, even. Like Singer in many ways.

Why, when Whitey had begun planning the Escape he'd told Felix—seriously—that nobody was to be hurt, *not even crew members.*

Felix had thought that very funny.

Just before he made contact with the bulkhead at the end of the corridor a sudden surge of acceleration sent him skidding into the wall. Clinging to a section of wall-net he watched his load roll for several yards, then lodge itself none too gently in a corner. The mental uproar from the passengers nearly drowned out the message from a relay somewhere in the vicinity who reported, "Captain had ordered half G acceleration for three seconds."

Now, Felix thought disgustedly, they tell me.

Singer, who was fluttering his wings slowly to compensate for the half G, hovered a few yards away. Anxiously, he asked, "How many more, Felix? There isn't much time left . . ."

"About a dozen Small Ones, and five of the others,"

Felix replied as the engines stopped and he began pushing his load through the open air-lock of the Test Rocket blister. "Relax. Two more trips should do it."

But Singer was the worrying type. Supposing Felix was caught at the wrong end of a corridor during a burst of acceleration. A fall of a hundred or more feet, even under quarter weight, would be bad for his passengers . . .

And it would be bad for him, too, Felix thought grimly. Possibly it would be fatal. He told Singer rather sharply to be quiet. Felix didn't like being reminded of all the unpleasant things that could happen to him.

Both test rockets lay in their slips. Blunt, grey torpedoes, their access panels lay open, and their stiffly-extended antennae made them resemble twenty foot beetles. Streamlining was unnecessary; the things weren't designed to break speed records, but to cruise about in the atmosphere of the planet being surveyed at a speed that wouldn't damage their sensitive testing gear, and possibly the even more delicate samples they would pick up from time to time. It was this low speed factor that had made the Escape possible. An ordinary missile, or even a message rocket, with an acceleration of fifty or sixty G's would have made a thin stew out of its passengers five seconds after blast-off. He thought the whole thing had depended on luck right from the start. The animals, apart from odd instances like the Communications Room death, seemed to get all the breaks.

Felix didn't like that. He was distrustful of too much good luck.

He gave his load a gentle nudge in the direction of the nearer rocket. It appeared deserted, innocuous, but Felix knew that inside it was a hive of activity. Most of the Small Ones from the nearby Seed Storage section—the 'wild' brethren of the Laboratory mice whose job was the provisioning of the rocket—were already in their positions. The rest were hidden at the open access panels waiting to take care of Felix's passengers.

"Here's another bunch of them," Felix thought at the apparently empty hull. He added lightly, "Fragile. Handle with care."

C

"Right," came the curt response. "We see them."

These particular Small Ones had no sense of humour at all where Felix was concerned, and with good reason. Before the Change had made them too smart to be caught, and before that same Change made Felix a reluctant vegetarian where live meat was concerned, he had hunted them a lot. During the early part of the voyage the carnage in Seed Storage had been shocking. They had never forgotten it, or forgiven him. Felix thought sometimes that living on a planet with the Small Ones wouldn't be much fun with a thing like that between them—he was becoming strangely sensitive about his bloody past—but when he thought of what the human minds were like at times . . .

Angry with himself for some reason, Felix kicked off on the first leg of his return journey to the Lab. He kept telling himself that he didn't care what the Small Ones thought of him. He didn't care at all. But he was an awful liar, he knew.

Transferring the remaining young to the test rocket was a simple, if strenuous job. There was only one point on the route that was dangerous—an intersection visible to anyone who might be standing in the entrance to the Control Room. But there had been too much going on in there for anyone to be hanging about the door, so they hadn't been spotted. Luck was still with them.

Felix waited beside Whitey, with an almost imperceptible weight pressing them against the wall. All around, the animals waited, too; not communicating, but thinking their own personal thoughts. He took what he hoped was his last look around the Lab. One of his cloth balls, he saw, had been stuffed with food from the robot dispenser—even though the Seed Storage people were supposed to handle the food supply end. Somebody was taking no chances. All the cages were open, and both of the ventilator grills above the door had been moved aside. As he watched, the door swung suddenly outwards and hung open under its own weight. The Small

One who had been working at the latch jumped free
and fell slowly across the room. They were almost ready
to go.

If a Human should look in here now, Felix thought, it
would be just too bad.

Weight disappeared again as the gentle deceleration
ceased. Seconds later a Small One in the tensely-waiting
crowd announced, "Relay from Control-room. Captain
has ordered kill engines. Orbiting manoeuvre completed."

To everyone in the room Whitey sent, "You know the
drill. Nothing can go wrong if we're careful, and if we
keep our heads. The relays will give warning if a crewman
intends coming too close to our escape route, minutes
before he arrives." Whitey was obviously thinking at the
Big Ones as he went on, "There are lots of places to hide
along the route if a Human should come—inside the
crew's life-suits, for instance—so there is no real danger if
you don't panic. Get to the rocket as quickly as possible.
And remember, you're on your own.

"The way is clear now. Move off!"

He added, "You first, Felix."

Felix sprang neatly through the Lab door, caught the
corridor wall-net, and sprang again. An almost-solid mass
of duncoloured animals erupted behind him and began to
pile up against the wall facing the door. He caught the
sharp, clear thought of Whitey cutting through the
growing confusion, trying to sort the mess out and get it
moving again. Felix didn't envy him his job.

Felix took up his assigned position—at the intersection
in sight of the Control-room—and waited. There were
men in there—he could hear low voices—but the range
was too great for him to catch their thoughts. They
couldn't have been important anyway, or the relay in
there would have passed them on. With a whole new
planet to examine, the crew were far too busy to think
about the laboratory animals—yet.

Eleven Small Ones came sailing along the corridor. They
landed against the wall-net almost as one, then launched
themselves on the next leg of their journey, still in that
tight formation. It was beautiful, Felix thought, but then

the Small Ones had had plenty of practice at weightless manoeuvring; besides, one of their greatest sources of pleasure was the execution of the most highly-complicated aerobatics to mind music. They were thinking serious, personal thoughts, but when he asked how the Big Ones were making out, one of them came out of it long enough to send him the mental equivalent of a snort of derision.

When Felix looked back along the corridor he saw what the other had meant.

A kicking, madly-struggling mass of Big Ones had just reached the end of the passage. A few Small Ones were trying to control the resultant pile-up, but without much success. It looked, Felix thought in awe, rather like a cloud of leaves being blown slowly up the corridor by a whirlwind. The Big Ones were moving fast, but they had no sense of direction at all—they kept bouncing *between* the walls, rapidly, and with a violence that made Felix wince. For every foot they moved forward, they travelled yards sideways, and even at this distance he could hear their panicky squeaking. Some of them definitely weren't keeping their heads. Suddenly worried, Felix sent to the relay near him, "Tell them to stop that noise, or the Humans will *hear* them."

There wasn't much danger of that just yet, of course. His ears were more sensitive than any Human's, but Felix didn't want to take any chances at all.

One of the Big Ones, more by luck than by judgement, came sailing up the middle of the corridor to land on the wall opposite Felix. Pleased, he began to radiate grudging approval, then caught what the other was thinking. "Don't!" he warned desperately. "Not that way—"

But he was too late. The Big One, disoriented and frightened by his trip, had already taken off from the wall, *and he was headed down the corridor leading to the Control-room*! Felix made some hurried calculations of direction and velocity, hoped fervently they were right, and took off after him.

Even with his stronger muscles giving him greater impetus, they were half-way to the Control-room door before Felix caught up with the other—and then he thought he was going to pass him. But with a series of convulsions that nearly broke his back he got close enough to grab a furry leg in his teeth. He hung on desperately as their different masses and velocities sent them spinning rapidly about their common centre of gravity. They smacked hard against the wall, only a few yards from the Control-room. Ignoring the frenzied struggles of the Big One, who was sure his leg was bitten off, Felix transferred his hold to the fur at the back of the other's neck and leapt back the way they'd come. He anchored himself solidly at the intersection.

"*That* way, stupid," he sent angrily, and with a strong jerk of his neck muscles he flung the Big One into the corridor leading to the launching slips.

Abruptly, he was sorry. There'd been no time for gentleness, of course, but he'd almost enjoyed mauling the unfortunate Big One back there. The other had been lost, confused, never been outside the Lab before. He shouldn't have ... Felix didn't quite know what he shouldn't have done.

"The thought does you credit, Felix."

Whitey had left the brown maelstrom that was boiling past the intersection, and was clinging to the net beside Felix. He had been in the thick of it, trying to keep the Big Ones moving—in the right direction, if possible—and he looked decidedly ruffled. He had been in collision with inanimate walls and over-animated animals alike more times than he could remember, and his nerves were beginning to suffer, too. Felix got all that from his mind in the brief pause before Whitey continued.

"That was fast, accurate thinking back there, Felix," he complimented. "You did very well—you can be proud of it. And when we reach the planet, you're going to do a lot better ..."

Suddenly uncomfortable and vaguely frightened at some formless meaning that was behind the other's thought, Felix interrupted hastily.

"Is that the lot?" He indicated a few stragglers floundering after the main group along the corridor leading to the rocket blister.

"Yes, that's all of the Big Ones," Whitey replied. "But the others have been told to wait for a bit. There's enough crowding and confusion as it is, and they, being Small Ones, can move quickly and hide more easily if they're spotted. They'll wait in the Lab until the Big Ones are safely aboard."

But Whitey wasn't to be put off by questions. Returning to his praising of Felix, he said, "You don't have to feel uncomfortable, Felix. Or frightened, either . . . but tell me, what do you think of the Big Ones? And what, in your opinion, makes them think and behave as they do?"

Felix thought that this was a fine time to start a philosophical discussion, but Whitey tactfully ignored that thought, so he began trying to explain how he felt about the slow, unbelievably impractical, but somehow likeable Big Ones. He didn't take long over it as he'd never really thought about them very much.

"You should have thought about them, Felix. You're wrong, completely wrong, in everything you think about them—" Whitey broke off as a straggler came crashing into the wall beside him. He reassured the frightened Big One, told him to take it easy, and sent him on his way again. Then he returned to Felix.

"They're definitely *not* stupid, Felix. Just slow to develop," he explained. "The Change is very gradual in them. With us Small Ones it was different—we Changed and reached our peak very quickly—in a few months, in fact. But now we've found indications that the Big Ones have a much greater potential I.Q. than we have—they are still changing. In a few months time, Felix, they will be our intellectual equals, *then they will pass us.*" There was no sign of rancour in the thought—Whitey was too highly-intelligent and civilized for that—only a great and burning excitement. "Think what this means, Felix. The size of their brains compared with ours . . ."

"No!" Felix was frightened, scared. He didn't want to think about it.

"But *yes,* Felix," The other contradicted. He stated solemnly, "You can't avoid the obvious. I am now certain that, barring accidents, you will eventually outstrip all of us. You will be the leader.

"If only," Whitey ended wistfully, "You weren't the only one of you . . ."

Felix felt suddenly that his brain had turned into a bubbling porridge and was about to squeeze from his ears. Fear and disbelief gradually gave way to belief, and an even greater fear—the fear of *responsibility*. But before he could form a coherent reply, another interruption drove everything else from his mind.

"Observation Room to Whitey," the relay in the corridor reported. "A Human has just left here. Intends walking in direction of launching slips. No fixed purpose—thinks he's in way of specialist crew members." The Small One stopped, awaiting instructions.

Three long, agonising seconds later, he was still waiting.

Felix had never known Whitey to behave like this before. The other's mind was a tight knot of fear and panic. It was an unforeseen and possibly tragic turn of events—just a sheer piece of filthy luck, but, Felix thought with a sudden feeling of pity, Whitey was behaving almost like one of the guinea-pigs.

Suddenly Felix remembered something; he took the initiative.

"Singer! Where's Singer?"

"Here, Felix." Singer was close by, only a few yards around the turn of the corridor.

"You heard that report." It was a statement, not a question. "You've got to intercept that Human, and stop him. Do the same as you did in Communications this morning—but get to him *quickly*. Follow the relay line to Observation, they'll give you his movements.

"And Singer, this is the most important job you ever had. Everything depends on it. You've got to stop that Human from coming here. The Big Ones aren't all aboard the rocket yet, and half the Small Ones are scattered over the Ship on relay duty." He ended grimly, "Stop him, Singer, if you've to peck his eyes out."

"Felix!" Singer was shocked again, but he got moving. Felix addressed Whitey:

"Better call in the relays. Singer may not be able to stop that Human, but if he delays him enough to get everyone to the launching compartment . . ."

To the relay beside him Whitey commanded, "Send this. To all Small Ones on relay duty and those waiting in the Lab. Move as quickly as possible to the launching slips—*now*. This supercedes all previous instructions." He paused, then went on to Felix alone. "You really meant that? About blinding the Human?" Horror, and a great sorrow was in the thought. "I cannot allow that, Felix, no matter what happens."

"*You* can't allow it!" Felix was exasperated. Angry yet somehow pitying, he went on, "Listen, You tell me I'm going to be boss eventually. Well, I'm taking over *now*—temporarily. You people aren't equipped to fight your way out of this, or anything else. I don't know how you'll be able to exist on the planet if one of its native life-forms decides to put up an argument—brains aren't everything you know. You're just too civilized for your own good. You wouldn't hurt a fly, even if not hurting it was to kill you." Felix became more and more heated as he continued, "With me it's different. You need someone like me to protect you. Someone who knows Humans well enough to be able to fight them. I ask you, would you let all your friends be caught and killed in lots of unpleasant ways, just to keep a Human from being messed up a little?

"Before *I'd* allow *that* to happen, I would kill that Human." He ended viciously, "There are ways an intelligent, trusted cat could do just that."

"Felix, you wouldn't . . . you *can't* take a life—even a Human life—like that." Horror, revulsion, and a terrible shocked urgency were in the other's thought. "Please don't think like that, Felix. Even injuring him . . ."

In ones and twos Small Ones were passing them, landing on the wall, and leaping towards the rocket compartment. They were the relays from all over the Ship, making for safety, escape. None of them paid any attention to the argument; they were too busy with their own thoughts.

". . . You wouldn't be able to live with a thing like that on your mind," Whitey went on desperately. "You think you could now. But later, when you've grown more intelligent, more sensitive . . . You're still a baby, Felix, a young savage, even if—"

One of the Small Ones passing broke in urgently, "Whitey. Singer's in trouble. Couldn't get details, the relay line is breaking up too fast, but it seems the Human got scared and took a swat at him. Broke his wing. Now the Human is taking him to Sick Bay to patch him up."

The Small One hurried on.

Felix used some thought, vocalisations that his old 'masters' would have envied. Then—

"To all Small Ones who can hear me," he sent as strongly as he could. "If you can get to the rocket within one minute, *move*! If you can't, *take cover*!"

Sick Bay was next door to the launching slips.

The corridor was suddenly empty as the Small Ones scurried for cover or the launching compartment. Felix knew that less than fifteen minutes remained before the rocket took off. And seconds before that happened, the access panels would close, the inner air-lock would seal itself, and a section of the Ship's hull would swing outwards—all automatically, and pre-timed to a second. If anyone wasn't aboard by that time, it would be just too bad. Felix knew what his own chances of making it were now that this latest crisis had been sprung on them, but he also knew that somebody should take control of the situation at the test rocket. Somebody smart—or in the confusion only a handful would get away . . .

He had no need to finish the thought. Whitey knew what was required.

"I'll go, Felix. But try to make it yourself. We're going to need you." Whitey tried to be commanding, but there was uneasiness in his thought as he reiterated, "And remember, Felix. I won't allow anyone to be hurt."

"I'll try," Felix replied hastily, "And there'll be no rough stuff unless it's necessary. Get going, Whitey. Good Luck."

The soft slap of sandals on the wall at the end of the corridor announced the arrival of the Human. The Man didn't notice the rapidly moving Whitey against the light grey paintwork; he came sailing nearer, still unsuspicious. As the other drew level with him, Felix leapt alongside with just enough power in his spring to keep pace with him. He was getting an idea.

The man reacted as expected.

"Uh-uh, Felix," the Human said harshly, "Don't touch," and hastily he transferred the unconscious Singer from his hand to the safety of the inside of his blouse. He was thinking that if Felix tried any tricks with the injured canary he would kick Felix the length of the Ship. The man didn't like cats.

So the crewman thought he wanted to get at the bird. Good; that was exactly what Felix wanted him to think.

As they drifted nearer the launching compartment, an urgent thought from Whitey told him that there were still a lot of animals milling about outside the rocket. Felix had expected that. He made contact with the wall-net and, just as the Human was approaching the open lock of the launching compartment, he sprang hard at the Human's chest.

He landed with considerable force beside that bulge that was the unfortunate Singer, sunk his claws into the fabric, and began screeching and spitting for all he was worth. Startled and angry, the Human tried to knock him off, all the time thinking of sneaking, treacherous cats trying to eat poor, defenceless birds. When Felix fastened his teeth into the other's sleeve—and into a piece of his arm, too—the Human began to get rough. It was quite a mêlée.

It ended when a vicious, open-handed smack sent Felix against the wall with a thump that nearly shook his teeth loose. But it had served its purpose; they'd floated past the open airlock without the Human seeing what was going on inside.

Feeling more dead than alive, Felix watched the crewman halt himself neatly at the door of Sick Bay. Once in there, Felix knew, even though the launching slips were only yards away, the animals would be safer, because the

Human intended to be busy working over Singer for some time. Maybe Felix would be able to make it to the rocket after all. The thought that Singer and some of the Small Ones still in hiding about the Ship would not make it had a dampening effect on his sudden rise in spirits. But, he told himself, he couldn't do anything about that.

The Human had the door open slightly, and was looking backwards over his shoulder to see that Felix wasn't going to sneak in, too, when he stared suddenly along the corridor. His jaw dropped open.

Felix felt the fur rise along his back. There was no need for him to follow the startled crewman's gaze—he saw what was happening with shocking vividness in the other's mind.

About twenty Small Ones had landed at the intersection at the other end of the corridor. Felix had forgotten about them; they were the ones Whitey had told to stay in the Lab, and because the relays had been called in, they'd had no knowledge of Singer's failure to stop the Human. Watched by the startled crewman, they took off again as they'd landed—in a tight, geometrically exact formation—in the direction of the launching room's air-lock. They must have seen the Human half-concealed in the door-way as soon as they jumped, but while rushing along the centre of the corridor in weightless flight there was nothing they could do about it.

Of all the blind, senseless, *lousy* luck. If it had happened just one second later the Human would have been safely in Sick Bay. But no. Bitter rage, born of despair, flared suddenly in Felix as he thought how near they'd been to escape—the gentle, impractical, too-intelligent Small Ones, and their slow, apparently-stupid, but likeable big brothers. But some of them could be saved yet—the ones already aboard the rocket—if Felix could force himself to act quickly enough.

The initial surprise in the crewman's mind had given way to an intense curiosity, and there was a slowly gathering suspicion as well. Felix knew he had to act fast. Deliberately he let his rage take root in his mind and grow. He could have controlled it at the start, but instead he fed it with memories, painful and humiliating incidents, anything at all that would fan it to greater heat. For what he knew he had to do Felix would have to be in the proper mood. He no longer trusted himself—or the soft, sentimental way he'd begun to think lately.

From inside the launching compartment Whitey's thought beat at him, desperately urging him to stop, to *think*. But it was like a cup of water on a forest fire. His rage mounted. Hazily he knew that the crowd of Small Ones had landed at the air-lock and that Whitey was giving them orders, but the thoughts didn't register. His rage grew to a blazing, white-hot fury, and his eyes never left the crewman.

The Human hung about ten yards away, with one hand holding the door and the other inside his blouse, defenceless. Vaguely, Felix knew that all the Small Ones were thinking at him now, but it had no effect at all.

For an instant he tensed for the spring, calculating, watching the Human's face. Then, with black murder in his heart, he leapt at the other's eyes.

He never reached them.

The mass and inertia of a moving Small One is inconsiderable, but twenty of them, leaping together and hitting him as one, was more than enough to deflect his dive towards the Human. Felix crashed into the wall-net amid a cloud of Small Ones, two feet away from the crewman. He was too shocked by the turn of events to move, but the Human wasn't. Kicking himself free of the doorway he drifted up the corridor, thinking that if he didn't get out of here quick he'd be drowned in living mice; and then thinking that mice shouldn't behave like that, and that Felix shouldn't . . .

Suddenly the Human's thoughts began to jump around. Instances, apparently unrelated, were linking up in his mind. Wires gnawed through, small components missing, tiny but important gadgets sabotaged. Could it be . . . Just then his jump carried him past the open lock of the launching compartment. He saw what was happening inside.

Felix hadn't realised how quiet it had been until the General Alarm siren blared out. Senses dulled with despair he watched the crewman jabbering into a wall phone and holding the Alarm button down with a hard-pressed palm. Voices began approaching from all over the Ship; excited, slightly frightened voices. Thoughts followed them as the crewman at the intercom broadcast his suspicions—the wary, coldly-implacable thoughts born in the brains of the most ferocious and deadly beast of all, *man*.

But, Felix knew, these beasts were logical. They would realise that they still needed experimental animals for the planets they hoped to find. They would not, be hoped fervently, slaughter all his friends right away.

But if they were too angry, they wouldn't behave logically.

Through the direct observation port Captain Ericsson watched a star that blazed like a gorgeous sapphire against a background of scattered silver dust. Home. He could almost see it coming closer. Smiling, he stroked the cat that sat on his shoulder, serenely following his gaze.

"Good thing your friends didn't make it to that first planet, Felix," he said reminiscently. "That virus... They wouldn't have lasted a week. But they should do all right on the world we picked for them. No animal life to speak of, a semi-intelligent plant-life to keep them from getting too lazy. Unless..."

Unless the gravity of their new planet brought about a reversal in the Change that had taken place in space, he was thinking. Even he didn't know for certain whether it was the prolonged absence of weight that caused it, or some enigmatic radiation given off by their home sun, Sol. That was why Felix had elected to remain on the Ship. A cat among a colony of mice, and guinea-pigs, and all of them degenerating... It wasn't a pretty thought.

As he addressed the others in the room, the tremendous being that Captain Ericsson had become used spoken words. They would be orbiting Earth in three days, and he wanted to become accustomed to communicating non-telepathically again. He said, "We are not going to like the Earth, even though it is our home. We've . . . outgrown it. The Change in we humans, with our larger and more complex brain structure, was very slow indeed—it took almost two years before our maximum development was attained. But even Felix here, who looks on us as near deities, is incapable of realizing just how much we have matured." He paused, shaking his head gravely. "No. It is our duty to report the habitable planets we've found, the Change that takes place in space, everything. And they will want some of us for psychological testing. But we will not like Earth. On Earth they fight, and hate, and do violence. They . . . they *kill*.

"I think we will want to leave again as quickly as we can."

Ouch!

PIERS ANTHONY

There's no reason to think that the inhabitants of other planets don't have toothache. But suppose you are landed with the job of curing it? If all your training and experience has had to do with human teeth, you are going to have to do a lot of very hard thinking—perhaps quite fast. Would you fare as well as the dentist in this story?

Dr Dillingham was forty-one years old: a conservative, successful, twentieth-century bachelor dental consultant. His acquaintances thought him unimaginative; his patients thought he overcharged; his pretty assistant was secretly in love with him. He was, in short, a typical dentist with a secure future.

As pride goeth before a fall, so may the typical go before the atypical.

Dillingham was not pleased to see Mrs Nostrand so early in the morning. She was overweight, her arches were fallen, her veins varicose, her manner insufferable. She seemed to be afflicted with most of the maladies imagined by man, with a single remarkable exception: she had virtually perfect teeth.

He wondered why she had chosen to inflict herself upon him. Possibly it was because every other dentist in the area had already informed her that however common dental restorations might be, they were dictated by the requirements of health, not fashion.

"Mrs Nostrand," he began, knowing it was useless, "no ethical practitioner is going to replace a healthy tooth with a substitute. Our purpose is to restore the mouth, as far as possible, to its original state of health. You should be gratified that you have no need of such service."

"But all my friends have genuine gold inlays!"

Dillingham controlled his temper. "I assure you, Mrs

Nostrand, they're not as good as nature's original dentin and enamel."

"Mrs Jones paid four thousand dollars for hers," she said enviously.

He turned away to conceal his disgust. Had it come to this? A running contest to see whose mouth could carry the most pointless wealth. . . .

"I'm sorry, Mrs Nostrand," he said with finality.

She stalked out, furious. He almost wished she *had* needed the work. It might have been easier to do it than to educate her.

Old Joe Krumpet, a too-regular client, was next. He was seventy and his teeth seemed to antedate the rest of his body: extremely old and worn.

" 'Nother blowout, Doc," he said cheerily. "Just put a patch on her and turn me loose."

Dillingham looked into Joe's mouth. It was sheer carnage. He wondered how the man could stray one bite from a liquid diet. There was hardly a disaster in the manual his teeth hadn't succumbed to over the years.

"Joe, that tooth will have to come out. There isn't enough of the original structure left to make it functional, and further deterioration could affect your—"

"Nope. None of that fancy stuff. Just plug her up so she don't hurt no more. She'll las' as long as I do."

He had a point there, unfortunately. Dillingham repaired the damage as well as he could, not even attempting to lecture the patient on oral hygiene. Joe Krumpet brought in his teeth for repair much as he would his vintage automobile. Who was a mere dentist to inject aesthetic complexities into his simple framework?

He finished with ten minutes to spare before the next appointment and retreated to his laboratory for a break. It was going to be one of those days: college kids who stuffed their mouths with sugar and looked blank at the mention of a toothbrush; businessmen who "hadn't time" to undertake precautionary hygienic measures; women so afraid of pain that they screamed when he brushed a healthy tooth with the mirror. All of them carelessly throwing away the priceless heritage of good teeth in their youth, heedless of the far more expensive and less comfortable substitutes necessitated in later life.

He was suddenly sick of it. Not of the work itself, but of the intolerable neglect he saw daily. So much of what he did would never be necessary if only people *cared*!

The radio was giving the routine details of another interplanetary space probe. Well, if there were other civilized creatures out there, surely they would long since have learned to preserve their natural assets! He visualized a baby bug-eyed monster smiling for the camera: "Look ma—no cavities for six generations!" Assuming bug-eyes monsters had teeth. . . .

He rose and returned to the operatory, knowing that efficient Miss Galland would have the third patient properly prepared. At least he was spared the interminable details. Sure enough, there was a figure in the chair.

As pride before the fall—

Dillingham put on his professional smile, washed his hands, and plucked a bright metal scaler from the tray. This was a new patient and—

He stared.

The face upon the headrest was alien. It was humanoid, but only vaguely so. A great flat forehead dropped down to widely spaced yet narrow eyes, and the nose was a triple slit. The mouth was closed, set off oddly by thin purple lips.

Before he could substitute a more appropriate expression for the frozen smile on his own face, there was a noise. He looked up to see a second creature fiddling with the locking mechanism of the door. The humanoid must have been standing behind the panel, waiting for him to enter. The features were similar to those of the reclining creature, but all Dillingham noticed at the moment was the visible hand. It was grey, and the fingers appeared to be double-jointed.

Dillingham tried to think of a clever remark that would dispose of the situation, but his mind remained awkwardly blank. What conceivable explanation could account for . . . ?

"Gentlemen, there must be some mistake, I'm a dentist, not a plastic surgeon."

D

Neither creature laughed. The one at the door straightened up and faced him silently.

Obviously he was the victim of an elaborate hoax. Nothing on Earth resembled these creatures. Someone at the local college must have set up this masquerade, fitting grotesque masks of that realistic flexible variety over their normal features. This was one of those disruptive pranks, funny only to the perpetrators. An initiation ritual. But how had they got past Miss Galland?

"Boys, I have a crowded schedule. Now that you've had your fun—"

The one in the chair opened his mouth.

Dillingham dropped the scaler to the floor. No mask could function as smoothly as this, yet the mouth was beyond credulity. the orifice was bone-dry and tongueless, and the teeth—

It was his business to know the normal and abnormal extremes of human oral anatomy. This far overreached them—but it was without doubt a genuinely functioning mouth, in a genuine functioning alien face. Since it was real, and no Earthly jaw contained dentures like these—

He decided not to ask questions whose answers might well be beyond his comprehension. This was no joke, and this was no longer a conventional problem. For some reason two aliens—extraterrestrial aliens, for all he knew—had come to his office to demand some service.

One sat expectantly in the chair. It could hardly be an accident. Why did anyone come to a dentist?

Somebody had a toothache.

The alien was not properly proportioned for the human recliner, but a few adjustments sufficed. Dillingham toyed with his instruments, wondering whether these creatures were dangerous. He couldn't afford to take a chance—

"Dr Dillingham," a voice called from the hall. The standing alien jumped, and something appeared in one hand. These two hadn't uttered a syllable so far, but they seemed to hear well enough.

"Dr Dillingham!" the voice repeated more urgently, and the knob turned. It was Miss Garland. "Are you in there? The door seems to be locked—"

The guard lifted his hand. He held a small object resembling a glass prism. He pointed it towards the door.

Dillingham didn't wait to find out what the prism was for. "I'm busy at the moment," he shouted, putting enough irritation into his voice so that she would realize it was important. "Something has come up. Please reschedule my next appointment."

Her soft heels retreated, and the alien lowered the prism. Perhaps there had been no danger—but it did seem best to keep the girl out of it until he could be sure. The aliens certainly seemed to mean business.

Did they use speech at all? The single glance he had had into the oral cavity gave him serious doubt that articulation as men knew it was possible. Still, there had to be some means of communication. . . .

Dillingham returned his attention to his patient. He seemed to be committed now, though of course he could not actually work on such a jaw. The mouth opened again and he surveyed it more thoroughly. It was a fascinating experience.

Four broad incisors lined the front section of the lower jaw, matched by five molars in the upper. This, at least, was what the teeth would have been called had they occupied a human mouth.

Biters opposed to grinders? Five to four?

What unearthly diet did this creature exist upon?

The overall problem of the alien presence became subordinate to the professional one. With dentition like this, how could he even guess at the normal state of the mouth? How would he detect the problem? And, granted a correct diagnosis, how could he ameliorate the condition? He knew nothing of the metabolism; he might kill the alien simply by applying a local anaesthetic. The creature might bleed to death from a single scratch—if it had blood. Nothing could be taken for granted.

The standing alien seemed impassive, but remained against the door, prism levelled. Suppose this were the captain of an alien vessel, and the patient a valued officer or crewman? It was convenient to think of these two as such, whatever the truth might be. Perhaps they had been on an exploratory cruise and had had difficulties that prevented an immediate return. Possibly their medical specialist had been incapacitated.

Whatever his reasons, the captain had seen fit to trust his man to the care of the nearest presumably competent specialist, rather than postpone the matter or handle it extemporaneously. The fact that the specialist happened to be of another world didn't seem to make enough difference to rule out the procedure.

There was food for thought here. Obviously the welfare of the individual was paramount, in the captain's society, surmounting even the formidable barriers between separate alien cultures. The individual who would trust a creature he had never seen before—an Earth dentist—to handle so precise and intimate a matter as the repair of an oral breakdown. . . .

That individual was either an absolute fool, or had enormous confidence in his control over the situation.

Dillingham glanced again at the captain. He did not have the aspect of a fool, and the prism glittered.

Yet the thing was impossible. The threat of a weapon could not create knowledge where none existed. It could not grant a human being the power to operate on alien metabolism.

The captain moved, gesturing with the prism. Dillingham immediately busied himself with the impossible.

The mouth was a paradox. There were no cuspids, no matched sets. Instead there were regular patterns of planed surfaces that could serve no conceivable masticatory purpose. The white units were obviously teeth of some kind, and firm pink gum tissue clothed the base of each unit, but the manner of the jaw's application was a tantalizing riddle.

Dillingham felt as though he were in a surrealist dream. Despite the intricacies of their derivation—teeth had first been formed from modified scales of the lip, countless millions of years ago on Earth—he knew them to be straightforward tools. They were required for any creature who cut, tore, crushed or ground its food, unless it specialized into some substitute, as birds had. There was no point in having teeth at all unless they acted in one or more of these ways, and cynical Nature neither evolved nor maintained superfluous organs. This alien's teeth had to be functional, even if that function remained a riddle to the dentist.

How was he to define the problem? He saw no evidence of decay or abrasion. Every surface gleamed cleanly white. While he was hardly in a position to make an accurate diagnosis, all the evidence suggested health.

He tapped an incisor experimentally. It was solid. All the teeth were firm and without blemish. Why, then, had this patient come?

Dillingham set down his instruments and stood back. "I can't help you," he said, trying to ignore the pointing prism and hoping his tone would put the message across.

The crewman closed his mouth, stood up, and went to the door. The captain handed over the prism and approached. Dillingham waited, uncertainly.

The captain took the chair and opened his mouth. Had they gone to all this trouble for a routine checkup?

Dillingham shrugged, washed his hands again, and brought out a sterile set of instruments. There didn't seem to be much he could do except oblige their whim. They *were* aliens, and it could be dangerous to cross them. He looked into the captain's mouth.

Suddenly it all came clear.

The crewman's mouth had been a healthy one. This mouth was not. The same peculiar pairings were present, the same oddly-angled occlusals—but several of the back teeth on the left side had sadly ravaged lingual surfaces.

The visitors had anticipated one of his difficulties, so had shown him the healthy set first, as a model. Now he did have some idea what was wrong.

"Dr Dillingham!"

The crewman whirled to aim the prism at Miss Galland's voice. Had half an hour passed so rapidly? "Emergency!" Dillingham called to her. "I'll be tied up all afternoon. Handle it as well as you can."

"Yes, Doctor," she replied with only the slightest hint of

disapproval. His present procedure was at best highly irregular; with a real emergency, he should have brought her into the operatory to help. Miss Galland was a highly competent dental assistant, but he tended to use her more and more as a receptionist because she made a much better impression on recalcitrant patients than he did. She really deserved to see this astonishing set of teeth—but he still did not dare expose her to the mercies of such questionable aliens.

Meanwhile, he knew that the problems entailed by his unexplained cancellations would be tactfully handled.

He probed the first of the damaged teeth: the second bicuspid, for want of anything resembling a properly descriptive term. The captain jumped; no doubt about its sensitivity. It looked as though some potent acid had eaten into the surfaces and stripped away the enamel and much of the softer dentin beneath (again applying human terms to the unhuman). It had been a recent accident; there was no sign of subsidiary decay. But the present condition was obviously uncomfortable and probably quite painful, and certainly constituted a hazard to health.

Dillingham observed that the buccal surfaces had also been etched. Only an X-ray, that he could not risk on the alien flesh, could establish possible penetration of the pulp. This was a rough case.

It might be possible for him to repair the damage, or at least cover it with a protective cast—but only if he could anaesthetize the jaw. Novocain was out of the question; any drug might be fatal.

The whole thing was ridiculous. "This is as far as I go," Dillingham said firmly. "I hate to leave you in pain, but my ignorance could kill you. I'm sorry." He crossed his arms and stood back.

When they saw that he was not going to proceed, the crewman levelled the prism at him again. The captain stopped that with a gesture. He stood up and recovered the instrument. He made sure he had Dillingham's attention, then aimed it at the wall and flicked a finger.

A spot appeared on the wall. Smoke curled up.

The captain made an adjustment and aimed again. This

time a portion of the wall exploded, leaving a charred hole.

He returned it to the first setting and pointed it at Dillingham. The message was clear enough.

But what would be their reaction if he botched it? Should he violate his professional ethics under duress? Dillingham shook his head, sweating. Perhaps they were bluffing.

"Dr Dillingham!"

Oh, no! Miss Galland had come back.

The captain nodded to the crewman, who whirled to unlock the door.

"Judy! Get away!"

"Doctor! What are you—"

Then the door was open and the crewman charged out. Judy Galland screamed.

Dillingham lunged at the captain, but the officer was ready. The beam from the prism stabbed savagely into his leg. Dillingham fell, clutching at the wound.

When the pain abated, he found Miss Galland standing beside him, her dark hair disarranged. The crewman had the prism again, and was covering them both.

"Doctor! Are you hurt?"

It was just like her to overlook the incredible in favour of the commonplace. She was not the fainting type, fortunately. He inspected his leg.

"Just a burn. It was set on low." He stood up.

The captain resumed his seat. The crewman aimed the prism at the girl.

So much for resistance. The show would go on.

"I don't think they mean any harm, Doctor," Miss Galland said. "They must be desperate." No hysterics from her; she had adapted to the situation far more readily than he.

Dillingham approached the patient. He had to quiet the shivering of his hand as he held a probe. Aliens, heat-beams—this was hardly the ordinary fare of a dentist.

But the problem of anaesthia remained. Massive excavation would be required, and no patient could sit still for that without a deadened jaw. He studied the situation, perplexed, noting that the crewman had put away the prism.

The captain produced a small jar of greenish ointment. It seemed that this contingency had been anticipated. These creatures were not stupid.

Dillingham touched his finger to the substance. There was a slight prickly sensation, but nothing else. The captain gestured to his mouth.

Dillingham scooped out a fingerful and smeared it carefully along the gingival surfaces surrounding the affected teeth. The colour darkened.

The captain closed his mouth. "How do they *chew*?" Miss Galland inquired, as though this were a routine operation. She had assumed her role of assistant naturally.

He shrugged. "The moment they take their eyes off you, slip away. We can't be sure of their motives."

She nodded as the captain reopened his mouth. "I think they're doing just what *we* would do, if we had trouble on some other world."

Dillingham refrained from inquiring just what type of literature she read during her off hours. He probed the raw surface that had been so sensitive before. No reaction.

So far, so good. He felt professional envy for the simplicity of the alien anaesthetic. Now that he was committed to the job, he would complete it as competently as he could. His ethical code had been bent by the aliens but not broken.

It was a full-scale challenge. He would have to replace the missing and damaged portions of the teeth with onlays, duplicating in gold as precisely as he could the planes and angles witnessed in the healthy set. While it would have helped immensely to know the rationale of this strange jaw, it was not essential. How many centuries had dentists operated by hit or miss, replacing losses with wooden teeth and faithfully duplicating malocclusals and irregularities? The best he could hope for would be fifty per cent efficiency—in whatever context it applied—yet if this stood up until the patient returned to his own world, it sufficed. There was no perfection.

Would a gold alloy react unfavourably with the alien system? He had to chance it. Gold was the best medium he had to work with, and another metal would be less effective and more risky. A good cobalt chromium alloy would be cheaper, but for really delicate work there was no substitute for gold.

He drilled and polished, adjusting to the odd internal convulsions, while Miss Galland kept the water spray and vacuum in play. He shaped the healthy base of each tooth into a curve that offered the best foundation. He bored a deep hole into each for insertion of the stabilizing platinum-iridium pins. He made a hydrocolloid impression of the entire lower jaw, since the better part of the reconstruction would have to take place in the laboratory.

Both aliens started when he used the hydrocolloid, then relaxed uneasily. Evidently his prosthodontic technique differed from that of their own world.

"Sorry," he said, as much to himself as to them. "Since I am not familiar with your methods, I am constrained to rely upon my own. I can't rebuild a tooth by guesswork."

"That's telling them," Miss Galland agreed.

He needed a model of both sides of the jaw because it was bilaterally symmetrical. A mirror-image reproduction of the right side might reasonably do for the left. He ignored the upper jaw. He knew nothing of the proper interaction of these surfaces, so the opposing pattern could only confuse him. He didn't want human preconceptions to distort the alien pattern.

But his curiosity about the way those incredible teeth functioned was hard to suppress.

He worked loose the hardened cast. He applied a temporary layer of amalgam, so that the jaw would not be sensitive when the anaesthetic wore off. Then he had to explain to the aliens by means of pantomime that this was *not* the end product of his endeavours.

Miss Galland brought a plaster model of human dentures, and he pointed to the cut-away teeth and lifted out the mock reconstructions, then gestured towards the laboratory. After several repetitions the captain seemed to get the idea. Dillingham led the way, with captain, Miss Galland and crewman following in that order. The major portion of the job was coming up.

Patients seldom saw the lab. Few of them were aware of

the enormous and precise labours that went into the simplest inlay, onlay or crown. This time, at least, he would have an attentive audience for his dental art.

Dillingham rinsed the impression immediately and immersed it in a two per cent solution of potassium sulphate while Miss Galland set up the equipment. There wasn't much else she could do, because special skill was required for the early stages.

The captain watched the routine with what Dillingham was sure was amazement. The aliens knew no more about the realities of dentistry than local people did! But what had they expected? Surely the techniques of North Nebula—to invent a home for the visitors—had points of similarity. Physical laws applied rigorously, whatever the language or culture.

He filled the impression with a commercial stone preparation, vibrated out the bubbles, and inserted the dowels and loops for individual handling of the teeth. While the die set, he simulated the remaining steps for the captain: the intricate wax mock-up of the onlay pattern for each tooth; the attachment of the sprue, so that the pattern and subsequent cast could be handled effectively; the investment, or formation of a durable impression around the wax pattern; burn-out, to free the investment of wax and leave a clear mould for the liquid metal; casting (he didn't even try to explain about the problems of expansion and contraction of gold and cast): and finally the pickling, finishing and polishing of each unit.

The captain's eyes seemed glazed, though the procedures were elementary. Here in the lab Dillingham was master, whatever the larger situation.

At last he manipulated the hands of the wall clock to show how many hours would be required for all this. He assumed that if the Nebulites knew enough about Earth to locate a specialist when they needed one, they should have mastered local timekeeping conventions.

The captain was not happy. Had he thought that an onlay was the work of a few minutes? Probably, like most patients, he hadn't thought about it at all. Everybody *knew* dentists spaced out the time between appointments merely to boost their exorbitant prices! Ha (brother!) ha!

The captain produced what appeared to be a hard plastic rod and chewed it meditatively on his good side. Dillingham was afraid at first that it was another weapon, but saw that it was not. Well, every species doubtless had its vices and mannerisms, and this was certainly better than chewing tobacco or gobbling candy.

The patient passed the rod to the crewman, who glanced at it with interest but did not choose to add any toothmarks of his own. No conversation passed between them, but abruptly the captain left. The crewman took a seat and kept the prism ready.

Evidently they did not intend to leave the captives to their own devices while the onlay was in preparation.

"They don't miss any bets," Miss Galland said ruefully.

Dillingham shrugged and bent to his work. It seemed that the surest way to get rid of the visitors was to complete the operation. He sawed his die into four separate segments, one for each damaged tooth, and plunged into the complex portion of the job. The wax he applied had to be shaped into the exact pattern of the desired cast. This, not the original tooth, was the actual model. The die determined the juncture with the living tooth, but the artistry lay in sculpting the upper surface of the wax into a serviceable and aesthetic duplicate of the healthy original.

He set the cruder plaster cast of the captain's jaw before him and began the most difficult construction of his career. It was not an image he had to make, but a *mirror image,* and his reflexes were hardly geared to it. Each of the four patterns would take several hours.

Night fell as he completed the second pattern. A new alien came to replace the crewman, but there was no chance to escape. They chewed sociably on rods, exchanged them, and parted.

"Dr Dillingham!" Miss Galland exclaimed. "That's how they talk! They make marks like that old wedge-writing."

It made sense. "Cuneiform," he agreed. That explained what the teeth were for! But the revelation, while satisfying intellectually, didn't help them to escape. The new guard was a vigilant as the first.

Night passed. Miss Galland slept on the emergency cot while Dillingham kept working. They both knew that help was unlikely to come, because the aliens had shown up on Friday and there would be no appointments for the weekend. Dillingham lived alone, and Miss Galland's room-mate happened to be on vacation. The captain had been quite lucky.

Something else occurred to him. "Miss Galland!" She sat up sleepily. "Since these creatures don't use sound to talk with, they probably don't associate it with communication at all!"

"Have you stayed up all night, Doctor?" she inquired solicitously. "You must be tired."

"Listen to me! We can plan our escape, and they won't realize what we're doing. If I can distract the guard's attention—"

She came alive. "Now I follow you. We could have telephoned long ago, if . . . but how can we get him to—"

He explained. They worked it out in detail while he poured thick jel around the wax and vibrated the cup. She slowly opened the windows, then set up a chair in front of one and sat down. One agile flip could tumble her into the back lot—if the guard were off-guard.

The work continued. The guards changed again, and the new one did not realize that the window was open. Dillingham poured melted gold into the inverted hollows of the final mould. The alien's attention was taken up by the sight of the hot metal; he knew that was dangerous.

"Now," Dillingham cried, as he plunged the hot cast into cold water. Steam puffed up, bringing the guard to his feet—and Miss Galland was gone.

Dillingham finished with a flourish. "How's *that* for a set of castings!" he cried. "Not to mention a slick escape," he added as the guard turned to discover what had happened. "The police will be here within half an hour."

The alien had been tricked, but he was no fool. He wasted no time in a futile chase after the girl. He pointed the prism at Dillingham, fired one warning beam that blasted the wall beside him, and gestured towards the door.

Two blocks away they came to an overgrown lot.

Hidden within the thick brush was a shining metal cylinder, large enough to hold several men.

"Now wait a minute!" Dillingham exclaimed as a port swung open. But already he was coming to understand that the clever alien captain had anticipated this situation also, and had come prepared.

The cooling onlays burned his hand. Perhaps the aliens had never intended to let the Earth-dentist go. If they needed help once, why not again, during the long voyage in space? He had demonstrated his proficiency, and by his trick to free Miss Galland he had forfeited any claim to mercy they might have entertained. The captain meant to have his restorations, and the job would be finished even if it had to be done en route to—

To where? The North Nebula?

Dr Dillingham, Earth's first spacefaring dentist, was about to find out.

* * *

The Enen—for Dr Dillingham preferred the acronym to "North Nebula Humanoid Species"—rushed up and chewed out a message-stick with machine-like dispatch. He handed it to Dillingham and stood by anxiously.

This was an alien world, and he was alone among aliens, but this was his laboratory. He was master, in his restricted fashion, and the Enens treated him with flattering deference. In fact he felt more like king than captive.

He popped the stick into the hopper of the transcoder. "Emergency," the little speaker said. "Only you can handle this, Doctor!"

"You'll have to be more specific, Holmes," he said, and watched the transcoder type this on to another stick. Since the Enens had no spoken language, and he had not learned to decipher their tooth-dents visually, the transcoder was the vital link in communication.

The names he applied to the Enens were facetious. These galactics had no names in their own language, and comprehended his humour in this regard no more than had his patients on distant Earth. But at least they were industrious folk, and very clever at physical science. It was surprising that they were so backward in dentistry.

The Enen read the translation and put it between his teeth for a hurried footnote. It was amazing, Dillingham thought, how effectively they could flex their jaws for minute variations in depth and slant. Compared to this, the human jaw was a clumsy portcullis.

The message went back through the machine. "It's a big toothache that no one can cure. You must come."

"Oh, come now, Watson," Dillingham said, deeply flattered. "I've been training your dentists for several months now, and they're experienced and intelligent specialists. They know their maxillaries from their mandibulars. As a matter of fact, some of them are a good deal more adept now than I, except in the specific area of metallic restorations. Surely—"

But the Enen grabbed the stick before any more could be imprinted by the machine's clattering jaws. "Doctor—this is an *alien*. It's the son of a high muck-a-muck of Gleep." The terms, of course, were the ones he had programmed to indicate any ruling dignitary of any other planet. He wondered whether he would be well advised to substitute more serious designations before someone caught on. Tomorrow, perhaps, he would see about it. "You, Doctor, are our only practising dental consultant."

Ah—now it was coming clear. He was a dentist from a far planet, ergo he must know all about off-world dentition. The Enen's naive faith was touching. Well, if this were a job they could not handle, he could at least take a look at it. The "alien" could hardly have stranger dentition than the Enens had themselves, and success might represent a handsome credit towards his eventual freedom. It would certainly be more challenging than drilling his afternoon class in Applications of Supercolloid.

"I'm pretty busy with that new group of trainees..." he said. This was merely a dodge to elicit more information, since the Enens tended to omit important details. Their notions of importance differed here and there from his own.

"The muck-a-muck has offered fifty pounds of frumpstiggle for this one service," the Enen replied.

Dillingham whistled, and the transcoder dutifully

printed the translation. Frumpstiggle was neither money nor merchandise. He had never been able to pin down exactly what it *was,* but for convenience he thought of it as worth its exact weight in gold: $35 per ounce, $560 per pound. The Enens did not employ money as such, but their avid barter for frumpstiggle seemed roughly equivalent. His commission on fifty pounds would amount to a handsome dividend, and would bring his return to Earth that much closer.

"Very well, Holmes. Bring in the patient."

The Enen became agitated. "The high muck-a-muck's family can't leave the planet. You must go to Gleep."

He had half expected something of this sort. The Enens gallivanted from planet to planet and system to system with dismaying nonchalance. Dillingham had not yet become accustomed to the several ways in which they far excelled Earth technology, nor to the abrupt manner of their transactions. True, he owed his presence here to an oral injury of one of their space captains, who had simply walked into the nearest dental office for service, liked what he found, and brought the dentist home. But there was a difference between *knowing* and *accepting.*

Dillingham was in effect the property of the Enens—he who had dreamed only of conventional retirement in Florida. He was no intrepid spaceman, no seeker of fortune, and would never have chosen such unsettling galactic intercourse. But now that the choice had been made for him—

"I'll pack my bag," he said.

Gleep turned out to be a water world. The ship splashed down beside a floating way station, and they were transferred to a tank-like amphibian vehicle. It rolled into the tossing ocean and paddled along somewhat below the surface.

Dillingham had read somewhere that intelligent life could not evolve in water, because of the inhibiting effect of the liquid medium upon the motion of specialized appendages. Certainly the fish of earth had never amounted to much. How could primitive swimmers hope to engage in interstellar commerce?

Evidently that particular theory was erroneous, elsewhere in the galaxy. Still, he wondered just how the Gleeps had circumvented that rapid-motion barrier. Did they live in domes under the ocean?

He hoped the patient would not prove to be too alien. Presumably it had teeth—but that might be the least of the problems. Fortunately he could draw on whatever knowledge the Enens had, and he had also made sure to bring along a second transcoder keyed to Gleep. It was awkward to carry two machines, but too much could be lost in retranslation if he had to get the Gleep complaints relayed through the Enens.

A monstrous fish-shape loomed beyond the porthole. The thing spied the sub, advanced, and opened a cavernous jaw. "Look out!" Dillingham yelled.

The Enen glanced indifferently at the message-stick and chomped a casual reply. "Everything is in order, Doctor."

"But a leviathan is about to engulf us!"

"Naturally. That's a Gleep."

Dillingham stared out, stunned. No wonder the citizens couldn't leave the planet! It was a matter of physics, not social convention.

The vessel was already inside the colossal mouth, and the jaws were closing. "You—you mean this is the *patient*?" But he already had his answer. Damn those little details the Enens forgot to mention. A whale!

The mouth was shut now and the headlight of the sub revealed encompassing mountains of flexing flesh. The treads touched land—probably the tongue—and took hold. A minute's climb brought them into a great domed air chamber.

They halted beside what reminded him of the white cliffs of Dover. The hatch sprang open and the Enens piled out. None of them seemed concerned about the possibility that the creature might involuntarily swallow, so Dillingham put that notion as far from his mind as he was able.

"This is the tooth," the Enen's message said. The driver consulted a map and pointed to a solid marble boulder.

Dillingham contemplated it with awe. The tooth stood about twelve feet high, counting only the distance it projected from the spongy gingival tissue. Much more would be below, of course.

"I see," he said, able to think of nothing more pertinent at the moment. He looked at the bag in his hand, that contained an assortment of needle-pointed probes, several ounces of instant amalgam, and sundry additional staples. In the sub was a portable drill with a heavy-duty needle attachment that could excavate a cavity a full inch deep.

Well, they *had* described it as a "big" toothache. He just hadn't been alert.

The Enens brought forth a light extensible ladder and leaned it against the tooth. They set his drill and transcoders beside it. "Summon us when you're finished," their parting message said.

Dillingham felt automatically for the electronic signal in his pocket. If he lost that, he might *never* get out of here! By the time he was satisfied, the amphibian was gone.

He was alone in the mouth of a monster.

Well, he'd been in awkward situations before. He tried once again to close his mind to the horrors that lurked about him and ascended the ladder, holding his lantern aloft.

The occlusal surface was about ten feet in diameter. It was slightly concave and worn smooth. In the centre was a dark trench about two feet wide and over a yard long. This was obviously the source of the irritation.

He walked over to it and looked down. A putrid stench sent him gasping back. Yes—this was the cavity! It seemed to range from a foot in depth at the edges to four feet in the centre.

"That," he observed aloud, "is a case of dental caries for the record book." The English/Enen transcoder printed a stick. He turned it off, irritated.

Unfortunately, he had no record book. All he possessed was a useless bag of implements and a smarting nose. But there was nothing for it but to explore the magnitude of the decay. It probably extended laterally within the pulp, so that the total infected area was considerably larger than that visible from above. What showed here was merely a vertical fissure, newly formed. He would have to check directly.

He forced himself to breathe regularly, though his stomach danced in protest. He stepped down into the cavity.

The muck was ankle-deep and the miasma overpowering. He summoned the sick dregs of his willpower and squatted to poke into the bottom with one finger. Under the slime, the surface was like packed earth. He was probably still inches from the material of the living tooth; these were merely layers of crushed and spoiling food.

He recalled long-ago jokes about eating apple-compôte, pronouncing the word with an internal S. Compost. It was not a joke any more.

He located a drier area and scuffed it with one shoe. Some dark flakes turned up, but nothing significant. He wound up and drove his toe into the wall as hard as he could.

There was a thunderous roar. He clapped his hands to his ears as the air pressure increased explosively. His foot slipped and he fell into the reeking centre-section of the trench.

An avalanche of muck descended on him. Above, hundreds of tons of flesh and bone and gristle crashed down imperiously, seemingly ready to crush every particle of matter within its compass into further compost.

The jaws were closing.

Dillingham found himself face down in sickening garbage, his ears ringing from the atmospheric compression and his body quivering from the mechanical one. The lantern, miraculously, was undamaged and bright, and his limbs were sound. He sat up, brushed some of the sludge from face and arms, and grabbed for the slippery light.

He was trapped between clenched jaws—inside the cavity.

Frantically he activated the signal. After an interminable period that he endured in mortal fear of suffocation, the ponderous upper jaw lifted. He scrambled out, dripping.

The bag of implements was now a thin layer of colour on the surface of the tooth. "Perfect occlusal," he murmured professionally, while shaking in reaction to the realization that his fall had narrowly saved him from a similar fate.

The ladder was gone. Anxious to remove himself from the dangerous biting surface as quickly as possible, he prepared to jump—and saw a gigantic mass of tentacles reaching for his portable drill near the base of the tooth. Each tentacle appeared to be thirty feet long, and as strong and sinuous as a python's tail.

The biting surface no longer seemed like such a bad place. Dillingham remained where he was and watched the drill being carried into the darkness of the mouth's centre.

In a few more minutes the amphibian vehicle appeared. The Enen driver emerged, chewed a stick, presented it. Dillingham reached for the transcoder—and discovered that it was the wrong one. All he had now was the Gleep interpreter.

Chagrined, he fiddled with it. At least he could set it to play back whatever the Gleep prince might have said. Perhaps there had been meaning in that roar. . . .

There had been. "OUCH!" the machine exclaimed.

The next few hours were complicated. Dillingham now had to speak to the Enens via the Gleep muck-a-muck (after the episode in the cavity, he regretted this nomenclature acutely), who had been summoned for a diagnostic conference. This was accomplished by setting up shop in the creature's communications department.

The compartment was actually an offshoot from the Gleep lung, deep inside the body. It was a huge internal air space with sensitive tentacles bunching from the walls. This was the manner in which the dominant species of this landless planet had developed fast-moving appendages whose manipulation led eventually to tools and intelligence. An entire technology had developed—*inside* the great bodies.

"So you see," he said. "I have to have an anaesthetic that will do the job, and canned air to breathe while I'm working, and a power drill that will handle up to an eighteen inch depth of rock. Also a sledgehammer and a dozen wedges. And a derrick and the following quantities of—" He went on to make a startling list of supplies.

The transcoder sprouted half a dozen tentacles as he talked and waved them in a dizzying semaphore. After a moment a group of the wall tentacles waved back. "It shall be accomplished," the muck-a-muck's reply came.

Dillingham wondered what visual signal had projected the "ouch" back in the patient's mouth. Then it came to him: the tentacles that had absconded with his drill and perhaps fragments of his other transcoder were extensions of the creature's tongue! Naturally they talked.

"One other thing: while you're procuring my equipment, I'd like to see a diagram of the internal structure of your molars."

"Structure?" The tentacles were agitated.

"The pattern of enamel, dentin and pulp, or whatever passes for it in your system. A schematic drawing would do nicely. Or a sagittal section showing both the nerves and the bony socket. That tooth is still quite sensitive, which means the nerve is alive. I wouldn't want to damage it unnecessarily."

"We have no such diagrams."

Dillingham was shocked. "Don't you *know* the anatomy of your teeth? How have you repaired them before?"

"We have never had trouble with them before. We have no dentists. That is why we summoned you."

He paced the living floor of the chamber, amazed. How was it possible for such intelligent and powerful creatures to remain so ignorant of matters vital to their well-being? Never had trouble before? That cavity had obviously been festering for many years.

Yet he had faced similar ignorance daily during his Earthly practice. "I'll be working blind, in that case," he said at last. "You must understand that while I'll naturally do my best, I cannot guarantee to save the tooth."

"We understand," the Gleep muck-a-muck replied contritely.

Back on the tooth (after a stern warning to Junior to keep those jaws apart no matter how uncomfortable things might become), equipped with face mask, respirator, elbow-length gloves and hip boots, Dillingham began the hardest labour of his life. It was not intellectually demanding or particularly intricate—just hard. He was vaporizing the contaminated walls of the cavity with the beam of a thirty-pound laser drill, and in half an hour his arms were dead tired.

There *was* lateral extension of the infection. He had to wedge himself into a rotting, diminishing cavern, wielding the beam at arm's length before him. He had to twist the generator sidewise to penetrate every branching side pocket, all the while frankly terrified lest the beam slip and touch part of his body. He was playing with fire—a fiery beam that could slice off his arm and puff it into vapour in one careless sweep.

At least, he thought sweatily, he wasn't going to have to use the sledgehammer here. When he ordered the drill he had expected a mechanical one similar to those pistons used to break up pavement on Earth. To the Gleep, however, a drill was a tapered laser beam. This was indeed far superior to what he had had in mind. Deadly but serendipitous.

Backbreaking hours later it was done. Sterile walls of dentin lined the cavity on every side. Yet this was only the beginning.

Dillingham, after a short nap right there in the now-aseptic cavity, roused himself to make careful measurements. He had to be certain that every alley was widest at the opening, and that none were too sharply twisted. Wherever the measurements were unsatisfactory, he drilled away healthy material until the desired configuration had been achieved. He also adjusted the beam for "Polish" and wiped away the roughnesses.

He signalled the Enen sub and indicated by gestures that it was time for the tank of supercolloid. And he resolved that *next* time he stepped off-planet, he would bring a trunkful of spare transcoders. He had problems enough without translation difficulties! At least he had been able to make clear that they had to send a scout back to the home planet to pick up the bulk supplies.

Supercolloid was a substance developed by the ingenious Enens in response to his exorbitant specifications of several months before. He had once entertained the notion that if he were slightly unreasonable, they would ship him back to Earth. Instead they had met the specifications exactly and increased his assessed value because he was such a sophisticated practitioner. This neatly added years to his projected term of captivity. After that he became more careful. But the substance remained a dentist's dream.

Supercolloid was a fluid stored under pressure that set rapidly when released. It held its shape indefinitely without measurable distortion, yet was as flexible as rubber. It was ideal for difficult impressions, since it could yield while being removed and spring immediately back to the proper shape. This saved time and reduced error. At 1300 degrees Fahrenheit it melted suddenly into the thin, transparent fluid again. This was its most important property.

Dillingham was about to make a very large cast. To begin the complex procedure, he had to fill every crevice of the cavity with colloid. Since the volume of the excavation came to forty cubic feet, and supercolloid weighed fifty pounds per cubic foot when set, he needed a good two thousand pounds.

A full ton—to fill a single cavity. "Think big," he told himself.

He set up the tank and hauled the long hose into the pit. Once more he crawled head-first into the lateral expansion, no longer requiring the face mask. He aimed the nozzle without fear and squirted the foamy green liquid into the farthest off-shoot, making certain that no air spaces remained. He backed off a few feet and filled the other crevices, but left the main section open.

In half an hour the lateral branch had been simplified considerably. It was now a deep, flat crack without offshoots. Dillingham put away the nozzle and crawled in with selected knives and brushes. He cut away projecting colloid, leaving each filling flush with the main crevice wall, and painted purple fixative over each surface.

Satisfied at last, he trotted out the colloid hose again and started the pump. This time he opened the nozzle to full aperture and filled the main crevice, backing away as the foam threatened to engulf him. He certainly didn't want to become part of the filling! Soon all of the space was full. He smoothed the green wall facing the main cavity and painted it in the same manner as the off-shoots.

Now he was ready for the big one. So far he had used up about eight cubic feet of colloid, but the gaping centre pit would require over thirty feet. He removed the nozzle entirely and let the tank heave itself out.

"Turn it off!" he yelled to the Enen by the pump as green foam bulged gently over the rim. One ton of supercolloid filled the tooth, and he was ready to carve it down and insert the special plastic loop in the centre.

The foam continued to pump. "I said TURN IT OFF!" he cried again. Then he remembered that he had no transcoder for Enen. They could not comprehend him.

He flipped the hose away from the filling and aimed it over the edge of the tooth. He had no way to cut off the flow himself, since he had removed the nozzle. There could not be much left in the tank.

A rivulet of green coursed down the tooth and over the pink gum tissue, travelling towards the squid-like tongue. The tentacles reached out, grasping the foam as it solidified. They soon became festooned in green.

Dillingham laughed—but not for long. There was a steam-whistle sigh followed by a violent tremor of the entire jaw. "I'm going to . . . sneeze," the Gleep transcoder said, sounding fuzzy. The colloid was interfering with the articulation of the tongue and triggering a reflex.

A sneeze! Suddenly Dillingham realized what that would mean to him and the Enen crew.

"Get under cover!" he shouted at the Enens below, again forgetting that they couldn't comprehend the warning. But they had already grasped the significance of the tremors, and were piling into the sub frantically.

"Hey—wait for me!" But he was too late. The air howled past with the titanic intake of breath. There was a terrible pause.

Dillingham lunged for the mound of colloid and dug his fingers into the thickening substance. "Keep your jaws apart!" he yelled at the Gleep, praying that it could still pick up the message. "KEEP THEM OPEN!"

The sound of a tornado raged out of its throat. He buried his face in green as the hurricane struck, tearing mercilessly at his body. His arms were wrenched cruelly; his fingers ripped through the infirm colloid, slipping. . . .

The wind died, leaving him grasping at the edge of the tooth. He had survived it! The jaws had not closed.

He looked up. The upper molars hung only ten feet above, visible in the light from the charmed lamp hooked somehow to his foot.

He was past the point of reaction. "Open, please," he called in his best operative manner, willing the transcoder to be still in the vicinity. He peered over the edge.

There was no sign of the sub. The colloid tank, with its discharging hose, was also gone.

He took a walk across the neighbouring teeth, looking for whatever there was to see. He was appalled at the amount of decalcification and outright decay in evidence. This Gleep child would shortly be in pain again, unless substantial restorative work were done immediately.

But in a shallow cavity—one barely a foot deep—he found the transcoder, undamaged. "It's an ill decalcification that bodes nobody good," he murmured, retrieving it.

The amphibious sub reappeared and disgorged somewhat shaken passengers. Dillingham marched back over the rutted highway and joined them. But the question still nagged at his mind: how could the caries he had observed be reconciled with the muck-a-muck's undoubtedly sincere statement that there had never been dental trouble before? What had changed?

He carved the green surface into an appropriate pattern and carefully applied his fixative. He was ready for the next step.

Now the derrick was set up and brought into play. Dillingham guided its dangling hook into the eyelet embedded in the colloid and signalled the Enen operator to lift. The chain went taut; the mass of solidified foam eased grandly out of its socket and hung in the air, an oddly-shaped boulder.

He turned his attention to the big crevice-filling. He

screwed in a corkscrew eyelet and arranged a pulley so that the derrick could act on it effectively. The purple fixative had prevented the surface of the main impression from attaching to that of the subsidiary one, just as it was also protecting the several smaller branches within.

There was no particular difficulty. In due course every segment of the colloid impression was marked and laid out in the makeshift laboratory he had set up near the waterline of the Gleep's mouth. They were ready for one more step.

The tank of prepared investment arrived. This, too, was a special composition. It remained fluid until triggered by an electric jolt, whereupon it solidified instantly. Once solid, it could not be affected by anything short of demolition by sledgehammer.

Dillingham pumped a quantity into a great temporary vat. He attached a plastic handle to the smallest impression, dipped it into the vat, withdrew it entirely covered by white batter and touched the electrode to it. He handed the abruptly solid object to the nearest Enen and took up the next.

Restorative procedure on Gleep differed somewhat from established Earthly technique. All it took was a little human imagination and a lot of Enen technology.

The octopus-tongue approached while he worked. It reached for him. "Get out of here or I'll cram you into the burn-out furnace!" he snapped into the transcoder. The tongue retreated.

The major section was a problem. It barely fit into the vat, and a solid foot of it projected over the top. He finally had the derrick lower it until it bumped bottom, then raise it a few inches and hold it steady. He passed out brushes, and he and the Enen crew went to work slopping the goo over the top and around the suspending hook.

He touched the electrode to the white monster. The derrick lifted the mass, letting the empty vat fall free. Yet another stage was done.

Two ovens were employed for the burn-out. Each was big enough for a man to stand within. They placed the ends of the plastic rods into special holders and managed to fit all of the smaller units into one oven, fastening them into place by means of a heat-resisting framework. The main chunk sat in the other oven, propped upside-down.

They sealed the ovens and set the thermostats for 2000 degrees. Dillingham lay down in the empty vat and slept.

Three hours later burn-out was over. Even supercolloid took time to melt completely when heated in a 1500 pound mass. But now the green liquid had been drained into reservoirs and sealed away, while the smaller quantities of melted plastic were allowed to collect in a disposal vat. The white investments were hollow shells, open only where the plastic rods had projected.

The casting was the most spectacular stage. Dillingham had decided to use gold, though worried that its high specific gravity would overbalance the Gleep jaw. It was impossible under present conditions to arrange for a gold-plated, matching-density filling, and he was not familiar enough with other metals to be sure they could be adapted to his purpose. The expansion coefficient of his investment matched that of gold exactly, for example; anything else would solidify into the wrong size because of contraction while cooling.

Gold, at any rate, was nothing to the muck-a-muck. Gleeps refined it through their gills, extracting it from the surrounding water in any quantity required.

The crucible arrived: a self-propelled boiler-like affair. They piled hundred-pound ingots of precise gold alloy into the hopper, while the volcanic innards of the crucible rumbled and belched and melted everything to rich bright liquid.

A line of Enens carried the smaller investments, which were shaped inside exactly like the original impressions, to the spigot and held them with tongs while the fluid fortune poured in. These were carefully deposited in the vat, now filled with cold water.

The last cast, of course, was the colossal vat-shaped one. This was simply propped up under the spigot while the tired crew kept feeding in ingots.

By the time this cast had been poured, twenty-four tons of gold had been used in all.

While the largest chunk was being hauled to the ocean inside the forepart of the mouth, Dillingham broke open the smaller investments and laid out the casts according to his chart of the cavity. He gave each a minimum of finishing; on so gross a scale, it could hardly make much difference.

The finished casts weighed more than twenty times as much as the original impressions had, and even the smallest ones were distinctly awkward to manoeuvre into place. He marked them, checked off their positions on his chart, and had the Enens ferry them up with the derrick. At the other end, he manhandled each into its proper place, verified its fit and position, and withdrew it to paint it with cement. No part of this filling could come loose in action.

Once again the branching cavern lost its projections, this time permanently, as each segment was secured and severed from its projecting sprue. He kept the sprues—the handles of gold, the shape of the original plastic handles—on until the end, because otherwise there would have been no purchase on the weighty casts. He had to retain some means to move them.

The derrick lowered the crevice-piece into the cavity. Two Enens pried it in with power crowbars. Dillingham stood by and squirted cement over the mass as it slid reluctantly into the hole.

It was necessary to attach a heavy weight to the derrick-hook and swing it repeatedly against the four-ton cast in order to tamp it in all the way.

At last it was time for the major assembly. Nineteen tons of gold descended slowly into the hole while they dumped quarts of liquid cement into a pool below. The cast touched bottom and settled into place, while the cement bubbled up around the edges and overflowed.

They danced a little jig on top of the finished filling—just to tamp it in properly, Dillingham told himself, for he considered himself to be too sedate to dance. He wished that a fraction of its value in Earth-terms could be credited to his account. The job was over.

"A commendable performance," the high muck-a-muck

said. "My son is frisking about in his pen like a regular tadpole and eating well."

Dillingham remembered what he had seen during the walk along the occlusal surfaces. "I'm afraid he won't be frisking long. In another year or two he'll be feeling half a dozen other caries. Decay is rampant."

"You mean this will happen again?" The tentacles waved so violently that the transcoder stuttered.

Dillingham decided to take the fish by the tail. "Are you still trying to tell me that no member of your species has suffered dental caries before this time?"

"Never."

This still did not make sense. "Does your son's diet differ in any important respect from yours, or from that of other Gleep tads?"

"My son is a prince!"

"Meaning that he can eat whatever he wants, whether it is good for him or not?"

The Gleep paused. "He gets so upset if he doesn't have his way. He's only a baby—hardly three centuries old."

Dillingham was getting used to differing standards. "Do you feed him delicacies—refined foods?"

"Naturally. Nothing but the best. I wish we had been able to afford such galactic imports when *I* was a tad!"

Dillingham sighed. "Muck-a-muck, my people also had perfect teeth—until they began consuming sweets and overly refined foods. Then dental caries became the most common disease among them. You're going to have to curb your child's appetite."

"I couldn't." He could almost read the agitation of the tentacles without benefit of translation. "Doctor, he'd throw a terrible tantrum."

Dillingham had expected this reaction. He had encountered it many times on Earth. "In that case, you'd better begin training a crew of dentists. Your son will require constant attention."

"But we can't do such work ourselves. We have no suitable appendages, externally."

"Import some dentists, then. You have no acceptable alternative."

The creature signalled a sigh. "You make a convincing case." The tentacles relaxed while it considered. Suddenly they came alive again. "Enen—it seems we need a permanent technician. Will you sell us this one?"

Dillingham gaped, horrified at the thought of all that garbage in the patient's jaw. Surely they couldn't—

"Sell him!" the Enen chief replied angrily. Dillingham wondered how he was able to understand the words, then realised that his transcoder was picking up the Gleep signals translated by the other machine. From Enen to Gleep to English, via paired instruments. Why hadn't he thought of that before?

"This is a human being," the Enen continued indignantly. "A member of an intelligent species dwelling far across the galaxy. He is the only dental consultant in this entire sector of space, and a fine upstanding fellow at that. How dare you make such a crass suggestion!"

Bless him! Dillingham had always suspected that his hosts were basically creatures of principle.

"We're prepared to offer a full ton of superlative-grade frumpstiggle . . ." the muck-a-muck said enticingly.

"A full *ton*?" The Enens were aghast. Then, recovering: "True, the Earthman *has* taught us practically all he knows. We could probably get along without him now. . . ."

"Now wait a minute!" Dillingham shouted. But the bargaining continued unabated.

After all—what is the value of a man, compared to that of frumpstiggle?

Evidence

ISAAC ASIMOV

When robots are so sophisticated that they are almost indistinguishable from human beings, how do you tell the difference? You can start by considering the three laws that all robots are programmed to obey:

1) A robot may not injure a human being, or, through inaction allow a human being to come to harm.

2) A robot must obey the orders given it by human beings except where such orders would conflict with the first law.

3) A robot must protect its own existence as long as such protection does not conflict with the first or second law. Perhaps you could then devise a test that would catch a robot out.

"But that wasn't it, either," said Dr Calvin thoughtfully. "Oh, eventually, the Jump through hyperspace was perfected, and now we actually have human colonies on the planets of some of the nearer stars, but that wasn't it."

I had finished eating and watched her through the smoke of my cigarette.

"It's what has happened to the people here on Earth in the last fifty years that really counts. When I was born, young man, we had just gone through the last World War. It was a low point in history—but it was the end of nationalism. Earth was too small for nations and they began grouping themselves into Regions. It took quite a while. When I was born the United States of America was still a nation and not merely a part of the Northern Region. In fact, the name of the corporation is still "United States Robots—". And the change from nations to Regions, which has stabilized our economy and brought about what amounts to a Golden Age, when this century is compared with the last, was also brought about by our robots."

"You mean the Machines," I said. "The Brain you talked

about was the first of the Machines, wasn't it?"

"Yes, it was, but it's not the Machines I was thinking of. Rather of a man. He died last year." Her voice was suddenly deeply sorrowful. "Or at least he arranged to die, because he knew we needed him no longer—Stephen Byerley."

"Yes, I guessed that was who you meant."

He first entered public office in 2032. You were only a boy then, so you wouldn't remember the strangeness of it. His campaign for the Mayoralty was certainly the queerest in history—"

*   *   *

Francis Quinn was a politician of the new school. That, of course, is a meaningless expression, as are all expressions of the sort. Most of the 'new schools' we have were duplicated in the social life of ancient Greece, and perhaps, if we knew more about it, in the social life of ancient Sumeria and in the lake dwellings of prehistoric Switzerland as well.

But, to get out from under what promises to be a dull and complicated beginning, it might be best to state hastily that Quinn neither ran for office nor canvassed for votes, made no speeches and stuffed no ballot boxes. Any more than Napoleon pulled a trigger at Austerlitz.

And since politics makes strange bedfellows, Alfred Lanning sat at the other side of the desk with his ferocious white eyebrows bent far forward over eyes in which chronic impatience had sharpened to acuity. He was not pleased.

The fact, if known to Quinn, would have annoyed him not the least. His voice was friendly, perhaps professionally so.

"I assume you know Stephen Byerley, Dr Lanning."

"I have heard of him. So have many people."

"Yes, so have I. Perhaps you intend voting for him at the next election."

"I couldn't say." There was an unmistakable trace of acidity here. "I have not followed the political currents, so I'm not aware that he is running for office."

"He may be our next mayor. Of course, he is only a lawyer now, but great oaks—"

"Yes," interrupted Lanning, "I have heard the phrase

before. But I wonder if we can get to the business at hand."

"We *are* at the business at hand, Dr Lanning." Quinn's tone was very gentle, "It is to my interest to keep Mr Byerley a district attorney at the very most, and it is to your interest to help me do so."

"To *my* interest? Come!" Lanning's eyebrows hunched low.

"Well, say then to the interest of the U.S. Robot & Mechanical Men Corporation. I come to you as Director-Emeritus of Research, because I know that your connection to them is that of, shall we say, 'elder statesman'. You are listened to with respect and yet your connection with them is no longer so tight but that you cannot possess considerable freedom of action; even if the action is somewhat unorthodox."

Dr Lanning was silent a moment, chewing the cud of his thoughts. He said more softly, "I don't follow you at all, Mr Quinn."

"I am not surprised, Dr Lanning. But it's all rather simple. Do you mind?" Quinn lit a slender cigarette with a lighter of tasteful simplicity and his big-boned face settled into an expression of quiet amusement. "We have spoken of Mr Byerley—a strange and colourful character. He was unknown three years ago. He is very well known now. He is a man of force and ability, and certainly the most capable and intelligent prosecutor I have ever known. Unfortunately he is not a friend of mine—"

"I understand," said Lanning, mechanically. He stared at his fingernails.

"I have had occasion," continued Quinn, evenly, "in the past year to investigate Mr Byerley—quite exhaustively. It is always useful, you see, to subject the past life of reform politicians to rather inquisitive research. If you knew how often it helped—" He paused to smile humourlessly at the glowing tip of his cigarette. "But Mr Byerley's past is unremarkable. A quiet life in a small town, a college education, a wife who died young, an auto accident with a slow recovery, law school, coming to the metropolis, an attorney."

Francis Quinn shook his head slowly, then added, "But

his present life. Ah, that is remarkable. Our district attorney never eats!"

Lanning's head snapped up, old eyes surprisingly sharp, "Pardon me?"

"Our district attorney never eats." The repitition thumped by syllables. "I'll modify that slightly. He has never been seen to eat or drink. Never! Do you understand the significance of the word? Not rarely, but never!"

"I find that quite incredible. Can you trust your investigators?"

"I can trust my investigators, and I don't find it incredible at all. Further, our district attorney has never been seen to drink—in the aqueous sense as well as the alcoholic—nor to sleep. There are other factors, but I should think I have made my point."

Lanning leaned back in his seat, and there was the rapt silence of challenge and response between them, and then the old roboticist shook his head. "No. There is only one thing you can be trying to imply, if I couple your statements with the fact that you present them to me, and that is impossible."

"But the man is quite inhuman, Dr Lanning."

"If you told me he were Satan in masquerade, there would be a faint chance that I might believe you."

"I tell you he is a robot, Dr Lanning."

"I tell you it is as impossible a conception as I have ever heard, Mr Quinn."

Again the combative silence.

"Nevertheless," and Quinn stubbed out his cigarette with elaborate care, "you will have to investigate this impossibility with all the resources of the Corporation."

"I'm sure that I could undertake no such thing, Mr. Quinn. You don't seriously suggest that the Corporation take part in local politics."

"You have no choice. Supposing I were to make my facts public without proof. The evidence is circumstantial enough."

"Suit yourself in that respect."

"But it would not suit me. Proof would be much

F

preferable. And it would not suit *you,* for the publicity
would be very damaging to your company. You are
perfectly well acquainted, I suppose, with the strict rules
against the use of robots on inhabited worlds."

"Certainly!"—brusquely.

"You know that the U.S. Robot & Mechanical Men
Corporation is the only manufacturer of positronic robots
in the Solar System, and if Byerley is a robot, he is a
positronic robot. You are also aware that all positronic
robots are leased, and not sold; that the Corporation
remains the owner and manager of each robot, and is
therefore responsible for the actions of all."

"It is an easy matter, Mr Quinn, to prove the
Corporation has never manufactured a robot of a
humanoid character."

"It can be done? To discuss merely possibilities."

"Yes. It can be done."

"Secretly, I imagine, as well. Without entering it in your
books."

"Not the positronic brain, sir. Too many factors are
involved in that, and there is the tightest possible
government supervision."

"Yes, but robots are worn out, break down, go out of
order—and are dismantled."

"And the positronic brains re-used or destroyed."

"Really?" Francis Quinn allowed himself a trace of
sarcasm. "And if one were, accidentally, of course, not
destroyed—and there happened to be a humanoid
structure waiting for a brain."

"Impossible!"

"You would have to prove that to the government and
the public, so why not prove it to me now."

"But what could our purpose be?" demanded Lanning
in exasperation. "Where is our motivation? Credit us with
a minimum of sense."

"My dear sir, please. The Corporation would be only too
glad to have the various Regions permit the use of humanoid
positronic robots on inhabited worlds. The profits would be
enormous. But the prejudice of the public against such a
practice is too great. Suppose you get them used to such

robots first—see, we have a skillful lawyer, a good mayor,—and he is a robot. Won't you buy our robot butlers?"

"Thoroughly fantastic. An almost humorous descent to the ridiculous."

"I imagine so. Why not prove it? Or would you still rather try to prove it to the public?"

The light in the office was dimming, but it was not yet too dim to obscure the flush of frustration on Alfred Lanning's face. Slowly, the roboticist's finger touched a knob and the wall illuminators glowed to gentle life.

"Well, then," he growled, "let us see."

The face of Stephen Byerley is not an easy one to describe. He was forty by birth certificate and forty by appearance—but it was a healthy, well-nourished, good-natured appearance of forty; one that automatically drew the teeth of the bromide about "looking one's age."

This was particularly true when he laughed, and he was laughing now. It came loudly and continuously, died away for a bit, then began again—

And Alfred Lanning's face contracted into a rigidly bitter monument of disapproval. He made a half gesture to the woman who sat beside him, but her thin, bloodless lips merely pursed themselves a trifle.

Byerley gasped himself a state nearer normality.

"Really, Dr Lanning . . . really—I . . . *I* . . . a robot?"

Lanning bit his words off with a snap, "It is no statement of mine, sir. I would be quite satisfied to have you a member of humanity. Since our corporation never manufactured you, I am quite certain that you are—in a legalistic sense, at any rate. But since the contention that you are a robot has been advanced to us seriously by a man of certain standing—"

"Don't mention his name, if it would knock a chip off your granite block of ethics, but let's pretend it was Frank Quinn, for the sake of argument, and continue."

Lanning drew in a sharp, cutting snort at the interruption, and paused ferociously before continuing with added frigidity, "—by a man of certain standing, with whose identity I am not interested in playing guessing games, I am bound to ask your co-operation in disproving it. The mere fact that such a contention could be advanced and publicized by the means at this man's disposal would be a bad blow to the company I represent—even if the charge were never proven. You understand me?"

"Oh, yes, your position is clear to me. The charge itself is ridiculous. The spot you find yourself in is not. I beg your pardon, if my laughter offended you. It was the first I laughed at, not the second. How can I help you?"

"It could be very simple. You have only to sit down to a meal at a restaurant in the presence of witnesses, have your picture taken, and eat." Lanning sat back in his chair, the worst of the interview over. The woman beside him watched Byerley with an apparently absorbed expression but contributed nothing of her own.

Stephen Byerley met her eyes for an instant, was caught by them, then turned back to the roboticist. For a while his fingers were thoughtful over the bronze paper-weight that was the only ornament on his desk.

He said quietly, "I don't think I can oblige you."

He raised his hand, "Now wait, Dr Lanning. I appreciate the fact that this whole matter is distasteful to you, that you have been forced into it against your will, that you feel you are playing an undignified and even ridiculous part. Still, the matter is even more intimately concerned with myself, so be tolerant.

"First, what makes you think that Quinn—this man of certain standing, you know—wasn't hoodwinking you, in order to get you to do exactly what you are doing?"

"Why, it seems scarcely likely that a reputable person would endanger himself in so ridiculous a fashion, if he weren't convinced he were on safe ground."

There was little humour in Byerley's eyes, "You don't know Quinn. He could manage to make safe ground out of a ledge a mountain sheep could not handle. I suppose he showed the particulars of the investigation he claims to have made of me?"

"Enough to convince me that it would be too troublesome to have our corporation attempt to disprove them when you could do so more easily."

"Then you believe him when he says I never eat. You are a scientist, Dr Lanning. Think of the logic required. I have not been observed to eat, therefore, I never eat Q.E.D. After all!"

"You are using prosecution tactics to confuse what is really a very simple situation."

"On the contrary, I am trying to clarify what you and Quinn between you are making a very complicated one. You see, I don't sleep much that's true, and I certainly don't sleep in public. I have never cared to eat with others—an idiosyncrasy which is unusual and probably neurotic in character, but which harms no one. Look, Dr Lanning, let me present you with a suppositious case. Supposing we had a politician who was interested in defeating a reform candidate at any cost and while investigating his private life came across oddities such as I have just mentioned.

"Suppose further that in order to smear the candidate effectively, he comes to your company as the ideal agent. Do you expect him to say to you, 'So-and-so is a robot because he hardly ever eats with people, and I have never seen him fall asleep in the middle of a case; and once when I peeped into his window in the middle of the night, there he was, sitting up with a book; and I looked in his frigidaire and there was no food in it'?

"If he told you that, you would send for a straitjacket. But if he tells you, 'He *never* sleeps; he *never* eats,' then the shock of the statement blinds you to the fact that such statements are impossible to prove. You play into his hands by contributing to the to-do."

"Regardless, sir," began Lanning, with a threatening obstinacy, "of whether you consider this matter serious or not, it will require only the meal I mention to end it."

Again Byerley turned to the woman, who still regarded him expressionlessly. "Pardon me I've caught your name correctly, haven't I? Dr Susan Calvin?"

"Yes, Mr Byerley."

"You're the U.S. Robot's psychologist, aren't you?"

"*Robo*psychologist, please."

"Oh, are robots so different from men, mentally?"

"Worlds different." She allowed herself a frosty smile, "Robots are essentially decent."

Humour tugged at the corners of the lawyer's mouth, "Well, that's a hard blow. But what I wanted to say was this. Since you're a psycho—a robopsychologist, *and* a woman, I'll bet that you've done something that Dr Lanning hasn't thought of."

"And what is that?"

"You've got something to eat in your purse."

Something caught in the schooled indifference of Susan Calvin's eyes. She said, "You surprise me, Mr Byerley."

And opening her purse, she produced an apple. Quietly, she handed it to him. Dr Lanning, after an initial start, followed the slow movement from one hand to the other with sharply alert eyes.

Calmly, Stephen Byerley bit into it, and calmly he swallowed it.

"You see, Dr Lanning?"

Dr Lanning smiled in a relief tangible enough to make even his eyebrows appear benevolent. A relief that survived for one fragile second.

Susan Calvin said, "I was curious to see if you would eat it, but, of course, in the present case, it proves nothing."

Byerley grinned, "It doesn't?"

"Of course not. It is obvious, Dr Lanning, that if this man were a humanoid robot, he would be a perfect imitation. He is almost too human to be credible. After all, we have been seeing and observing human beings all our lives; it would be impossible to palm something merely nearly right off on us. It would have to be *all* right. Observe the texture of the skin, the quality of the irises, the bone formation of the hand. If he's a robot, I wish U.S. Robots *had* made him, because he's a good job. Do you suppose then, that anyone capable of paying attention to such niceties would neglect a few gadgets to take care of such things as eating, sleeping, elimination? For emergency use only, perhaps; as, for instance, to prevent such situations as are rising here. So a meal won't prove anything."

"Now wait," snarled Lanning, "I am not quite the fool

both of you make me out to be. I am not interested in the problem of Mr Byerley's humanity or nonhumanity. I am interested in getting the corporation out of a hole. A public meal will end the matter and keep it ended no matter what Quinn does. We can leave the finer details to lawyers and robopsychologists."

"But, Dr Lanning," said Byerley, "you forget the politics of the situation. I am as anxious to be elected, as Quinn is to stop me. By the way, did you notice that you used his name? It's a cheap shyster trick of mine; I knew you would, before you were through."

Lanning flushed, "What has the election to do with it?"

"Publicity works both ways, sir. If Quinn wants to call me a robot, and has the nerve to do so, I have the nerve to play the game his way."

"You mean you—" Lanning was quite frankly appalled.

"Exactly. I mean that I'm going to let him go ahead, choose his rope, test its strength, cut off the right length, tie the noose, insert his head and grin. I can do what little else is required."

"You are mighty confident."

Susan Calvin rose to her feet, "Come, Alfred, we won't change his mind for him."

"You see." Byerley smiled gently. "You're a human psychologist, too."

But perhaps not all the confidence that Dr Lanning had remarked upon was present that evening when Byerley's car parked on the automatic treads leading to the sunken garage, and Byerley himself crossed the path to the front door of his house.

The figure in the wheel chair looked up as he entered and smiled. Byerley's face lit with affection. He crossed over to it.

The cripple's voice was a hoarse, grating whisper that came out of a mouth forever twisted to one side, leering out of a face that was half scar tissue, "You're late, Steve."

"I know, John, I know. But I've been up against a peculiar and interesting trouble today."

"So?" Neither the torn face nor the destroyed voice

could carry expression but there was anxiety in the clear
eyes. "Nothing you can't handle?"

"I'm not exactly certain. I may need your help. *You're*
the brilliant one in the family. Do you want me to take you
out into the garden? It's a beautiful evening."

Two strong arms lifted John from the wheel chair.
Gently, almost caressingly, Byerley's arms went around the
shoulders and under the swathed legs of the cripple.
Carefully, and slowly, he walked through the rooms, down
the gentle ramp that had been built with a wheel chair in
mind, and out the back door into the walled and wired
garden behind the house.

"Why don't you let me use the wheel chair, Steve? This
is silly."

"Because I'd rather carry you. Do you object? You
know that you're as glad to get out of that motorized
buggy for a while as I am to see you out. How do you feel
today?" He deposited John with infinite care upon the cool
grass.

"How should I feel? But tell me about your trouble."

"Quinn's campaign will be based on the fact that he
claims I'm a robot."

John's eyes opened wide, "How do you know? It's
impossible. I won't believe it."

"Oh, come, I tell you it's so. He had one of the big-shot
scientists of U.S. Robot & Mechanical Men Corporation
over at the office to argue with me."

Slowly John's hands tore at the grass, "I see. I see."

Byerley said, "But we can let him choose his ground. I
have an idea. Listen to me and tell me if we can do it—"

The scene as it appeared in Alfred Lanning's office that
night was a tableau of stares. Francis Quinn stared
meditatively at Alfred Lanning. Lanning's stare was
savagely set upon Susan Calvin, who stared impassively in
her turn at Quinn.

Francis Quinn broke it with a heavy attempt at lightness,
"Bluff. He's making it up as he goes along."

"Are you going to gamble on that, Mr Quinn?" asked
Dr Calvin, indifferently.

"Well, it's your gamble, really."

"Look here," Lanning covered definite pessimism with bluster, "we've done what you asked. We witnessed the man eat. It's ridiculous to presume him a robot."

"Do *you* think so?" Quinn shot toward Calvin. "Lanning said you were the expert."

Lanning was almost threatening, "Now, Susan—"

Quinn interrupted smoothly, "Why not let her talk, man? She's been sitting there imitating a gatepost for half an hour."

Lanning felt definitely harassed. From what he experienced then to incipient paranoia was but a step. He said, "Very well. Have your say, Susan. We won't interrupt you."

Susan Calvin glanced at him humourlessly, then fixed cold eyes on Mr Quinn. "There are only two ways of definitely proving Byerley to be a robot, sir. So far you are presenting circumstantial evidence, with which you can accuse, but not prove—and I think Mr Byerley is sufficiently clever to counter that sort of material. You probably think so yourself, or you wouldn't have come here.

"The two methods of *proof* are the physical and the psychological. Physically, you can dissect him or use an X-ray. How to do that would be *your* problem. Psychologically, his behavior can be studied, for if he *is* a positronic robot, he must conform to the three Rules of Robotics. A positronic brain cannot be constructed without them. You know the Rules, Mr Quinn?"

She spoke them carefully, clearly, quoting word for word the famous bold print on page one of the *Handbook of Robotics*.

"I've heard of them," said Quinn, carelessly.

"Then the matter is easy to follow," responded the psychologist, dryly. "If Mr Byerley breaks any of those three rules, he is not a robot. Unfortunately, this procedure works in only one direction. If he lives up to the rules, it proves nothing one way or the other."

Quinn raised polite eyebrows, "Why not, doctor?"

"Because, if you stop to think of it, the three Rules of Robotics are the essential guiding principles of a good

many of the world's ethical systems. Of course, every
human being is supposed to have the instinct of self-
preservation. That's Rule Three to a robot. Also every
'good' human being, with a social conscience and a sense of
responsibility, is supposed to defer to proper authority; to
listen to his doctor, his boss, his government, his
psychiatrist, his fellow man; to obey laws, to follow rules,
to conform to custom—even when they interfere with his
comfort or his safety. That's Rule Two to a robot. Also,
every 'good' human being is supposed to love others as
himself, protect his fellow man, risk his life to save another.
That's Rule One to a robot. To put it simply—if Byerley
follows all the Rules of Robotics, he may be a robot, and
may simply be a very good man."

"But," said Quinn, "you're telling me that you can never
prove him a robot."

"I may be able to prove him *not* a robot."

"That's not the proof I want."

"You'll have such proof as exists. You are the only one
responsible for your own wants."

Here Lanning's mind leaped suddenly to the sting of an
idea, "Has it occurred to anyone," he ground out, "that
district attorney is a rather strange occupation for a robot?
The prosecution of human beings—sentencing them to
death—bringing about their infinite harm—"

Quinn grew suddenly keen, "No, you can't get out of it
that way. Being district attorney doesn't make him human.
Don't you know his record? Don't you know that he
boasts that he has never prosecuted an innocent man; that
there are scores of people left untried because the evidence
against them didn't satisfy him, even though he could
probably have argued a jury into atomizing them? That
happens to be so."

Lanning's thin cheeks quivered, "No, Quinn, no. There
is nothing in the Rules of Robotics that makes any
allowance for human guilt. A robot may not judge whether
a human being deserves death. It is not for him to decide.
He may not harm a human—variety skunk, or variety
angel."

Susan Calvin sounded tired. "Alfred," she said, "don't talk foolishly. What if a robot came upon a madman about to set fire to a house with people in it. He would stop the madman, wouldn't he?"

"Of course."

"And if the only way he could stop him was to kill him—"

There was a faint sound in Lanning's throat. Nothing more.

"The answer to that, Alfred, is that he would do his best not to kill him. If the madman died, the robot would require psychotherapy because he might easily go mad at the conflict presented him—of having broken Rule One to adhere to Rule One in a higher sense. But a man would be dead and a robot would have killed him."

"Well, *is* Byerley mad?" demanded Lanning, with all the sarcasm he could muster.

"No, but he has killed no man himself. He has exposed facts which might represent a particular human being to be dangerous to the large mass of other human beings we call society. He protects the greater number and thus adheres to Rule One at maximum potential. That is as far as he goes. It is the judge who then condemns the criminal to death or imprisonment, after the jury decides on his guilt or innocence. It is the jailer who imprisons him, the executioner who kills him. and Mr Byerley has done nothing but determine truth and aid society.

"As a matter of fact, Mr Quinn, I have looked into Mr Byerley's career since you first brought this matter to our attention. I find that he has never demanded the death sentence in his closing speeches to the jury. I also find that he has spoken on behalf of the abolition of capital punishment and contributed generously to research institutions engaged in criminal neurophysiology. He apparently believes in the cure, rather than the punishment of crime. I find that significant."

"You do?" Quinn smiled. "Significant of a certain odor of roboticity, perhaps?"

"Perhaps. Why deny it? Actions such as his could come only from a robot, or from a very honourable and decent human being. But you see, you just can't differentiate between a robot and the very best of humans."

Quinn sat back in his chair. His voice quivered with impatience. "Dr Lanning, it's perfectly possible to create a humanoid robot that would perfectly duplicate a human in appearance, isn't it?"

Lanning harrumphed and considered, "It's been done experimentally by U.S. Robots," he said reluctantly, "without the addition of a positronic brain, of course. By using human ova and hormone control, one can grow human flesh and skin over a skeleton of porous silicone plastics that would defy external examination. The eyes, the hair, the skin would be really human, not humanoid. and if you put a positronic brain, and such other gadgets as you might desire inside, you have a humanoid robot."

Quinn said shortly, "How long would it take to make one?"

Lanning considered, "If you had all your equipment—the brain, the skeleton, the ovum, the proper hormones and radiations—say, two months."

The politician straightened out of his chair. "Then we shall see what the insides of Mr Byerley look like. It will mean publicity for U.S. Robots—but I gave you your chance."

Lanning turned impatiently to Susan Calvin, when they were alone. "Why do you insist—"

And with real feeling, she responded sharply and instantly, "Which do you want—the truth or my resignation? I won't lie for you. U.S. Robots can take care of itself. Don't turn coward."

"What," said Lanning, "if he opens up Byerley, and wheels and gears fall out. What then?"

"He won't open Byerley," said Calvin, disdainfully. "Byerley is as clever as Quinn, at the very least."

The news broke upon the city a week before Byerley was to have been nominated. But "broke" is the wrong word. It staggered upon the city, shambled, crawled. Laughter began, and wit was free. And as the far off hand of Quinn tightened its pressure in easy stages, the laughter grew forced, an element of hollow uncertainty entered, and people broke off to wonder.

The convention itself had the air of a restive stallion. There had been no contest planned. Only Byerley could possibly have been nominated a week earlier. There was no substitute even now. They had to nominate him, but there was complete confusion about it.

It would not have been so bad if the average individual were not torn between the enormity of the charge, if true, and its sensational folly, if false.

The day after Byerley was nominated perfunctorily, hollowly—a newspaper finally published the gist of a long interview with Dr Susan Calvin, "world famous expert on robopsychology and positronics."

What broke loose is popularly and succinctly described as hell.

It was what the Fundamentalists were waiting for. They were not a political party; they made pretence to no formal religion. Essentially they were those who had not adapted themselves to what had once been called the Atomic Age, in the days when atoms were a novelty. Actually, they were the Simple-Lifers, hungering after a life, which to those who lived it had probably appeared not so Simple, and who had been, therefore, Simple-Lifers themselves.

The Fundamentalists required no new reason to detest robots and robot manufacturers; but a new reason such as the Quinn accusation and the Calvin analysis was sufficient to make such detestation audible.

The huge plants of the U.S. Robot & Mechanical Men Corporation was a hive that spawned armed guards. It prepared for war.

Within the city the house of Stephen Byerley bristled with police.

The political campaign, of course, lost all other issues, and resembled a campaign only in that it was something filling the hiatus between nomination and election.

Stephen Byerley did not allow the fussy little man to distract him. He remained comfortably unperturbed by the uniforms in the background. Outside the house, past the line of grim guards, reporters and photographers waited according to the tradition of the caste. One enterprising 'visor station even had a scanner focused on the blank entrance to the prosecutor's unpretentious home, while a synthetically excited announcer filled in with inflated commentary.

The fussy little man advanced. He held forward a rich, complicated sheet. "This, Mr Byerley, is a court order authorizing me to search these premises for the presence of illegal . . . uh . . . mechanical men or robots of any description."

Byerley half rose, and took the paper. He glanced at it indifferently, and smiled as he handed it back. "All in order. Go ahead. Do your job. Mrs Hoppen"—to his housekeeper, who appeared reluctantly from the next room—"please go with them, and help out if you can."

The little man, whose name was Harroway, hesitated, produced an unmistakable blush, failed completely to catch Byerley's eyes, and muttered, "Come on," to the two policemen.

He was back in ten minutes.

"Through?" questioned Byerley, in just the tone of a person who is not particularly interested in the question, or its answer.

Harroway cleared his throat, made a bad start in falsetto, and began again, angrily, "Look here, Mr Byerley, our special instructions were to search the house very thoroughly."

"And haven't you?"

"We were told exactly what to look for."

"Yes?"

"In short, Mr Byerley, and not to put too fine a point on it, we were told to search you."

"Me?" said the prosecutor with a broadening smile. "And how do you intend to do that?"

"We have a Penet-radiation unit—"

"Then I'm to have my X-ray photograph taken, hey? You have the authority?"

"You saw my warrant."

"May I see it again?"

Harroway, his forehead shining with considerably more than mere enthusiasm, passed it over a second time.

Byerley said evenly, "I read here as the description of what you are to search; I quote: 'the dwelling place belonging to Stephen Allen Byerley, located at 355 Willow Grove, Evanstron, together with any garage, storehouse or other structures or buildings thereto appertaining, together with all grounds thereto appertaining' . . . um . . . and so on. Quite in order. But, my good man, it doesn't say anything about searching my interior. I am not part of the premises. You may search my clothes if you think I've got a robot hidden in my pocket."

Harroway had no doubt on the point of to whom he owed his job. He did not propose to be backward, given a chance to earn a much better—i.e., more highly paid—job.

He said, in a faint echo of bluster, "Look here. I'm allowed to search the furniture in your house, and anything else I find in it. You are in it, aren't you?"

"A remarkable observation. I *am* in it. But I'm not a piece of furniture. As a citizen of adult responsibility—I have the psychiatric certificate proving that—I have certain rights under the Regional Articles. Searching me would come under the heading of violating my Right of Privacy. That paper isn't sufficient."

"Sure, but if you're a robot, you don't have Right of Privacy."

"True enough—but that paper still isn't sufficient. It recognizes me implicitly as a human being."

"Where?" Harroway snatched at it.

"Where it says 'the dwelling place belonging to' and so on. A robot cannot own property. and you may tell your employer, Mr Harroway, that if he tries to issue a similar paper which does *not* implicitly recognize me as a human being, he will be immediately faced with a restraining injunction and a civil suit which will make it necessary for him to *prove* me a robot by means of information *now* in his possession, or else to pay a whopping penalty for an attempt to deprive me unduly of my Rights under the Regional Articles. You'll tell him that, won't you?"

Harroway marched to the door. He turned. "You're a

slick lawyer—" His hand was in his pocket. For a short moment, he stood there. Then he left, smiled in the direction of the 'visor scanner, still playing away—waved to the reporters, and shouted, "We'll have something for you tomorrow, boys. No kidding."

In his ground car, he settled back, removed the tiny mechanism from his pocket and carefully inspected it. It was the first time he had ever taken a photograph by X-ray reflection. He hoped he had done it correctly.

Quinn and Byerley had never met face-to-face alone. But visorphone was pretty close to it. In fact, accepted literally, perhaps the phrase was accurate, even if to each, the other were merely the light and dark pattern of a bank of photocells.

It was Quinn who had initiated the call. It was Quinn, who spoke first, and without particular ceremony, "Thought you would like to know, Byerley, that I intend to make public the fact that you're wearing a protective shield against Penet-radiation."

"That so? In that case, you've probably already made it public. I have a notion our enterprising press representatives have been tapping my various communication lines for quite a while. I know they have my office lines full of holes; which is why I've dug in at my home these last weeks." Byerley was friendly, almost chatty.

Quinn's lips tightened slightly, "This call is shielded—thoroughly. I'm making it at a certain personal risk."

"So I should imagine. Nobody knows you're behind this campaign. At least, nobody knows it officially. Nobody doesn't know it unofficially. I wouldn't worry. So I wear a protective shield? I suppose you found that out when your puppy dog's Penet-radiation photograph, the other day, turned out to be over-exposed."

"You realize, Byerley, that it would be pretty obvious to everyone that you don't dare face X-ray analysis."

"Also that you, or your men, attempted illegal invasion of my Right of Privacy."

"The devil they'll care for that."

"They might. It's rather symbolic of our two campaigns, isn't it? You have little concern with the rights of the individual citizen. I have great concern. I will not submit to X-ray analysis, because I wish to maintain my Rights on principle. Just as I'll maintain the rights of others when elected."

"That will no doubt make a very interesting speech, but no one will believe you. A little too high-sounding to be true. Another thing," a sudden, crisp change, "the personnel in your home was not complete the other night."

"In what way?"

"According to the report," he shuffled papers before him that were just within the range of vision of the visiplate, "there was one person missing—a cripple."

"As you say," said Byerley, tonelessly, "a cripple. My old teacher, who lives with me and who is now in the country—and has been for two months. A 'much-needed rest' is the usual expression applied in the case. He has your permission?"

"Your teacher? A scientist of sorts?"

"A lawyer once—before he was a cripple. He has a government licence as a research biophysicist, with a laboratory of his own, and a complete description of the work he's doing filed with the proper authorities, to whom I can refer you. The work is minor, but is a harmless and engaging hobby for a—poor cripple. I am being as helpful as I can, you see."

"I see. And what does this... teacher... know about robot manufacture?"

"I couldn't judge the extent of his knowledge in a field with which I am unacquainted."

"He wouldn't have access to positronic brains?"

"Ask your friends at U.S. Robots. They'd be the ones to know."

"I'll put it shortly, Byerley. Your crippled teacher is the real Stephen Byerley. You are his robot creation. We can prove it. It was he who was in the automobile accident, not you. There will be ways of checking the records."

"Really? Do so, then. My best wishes."

"And we can search your so-called teacher's 'country

G

place', and see what we can find there."

"Well, not quite, Quinn." Byerley smiled broadly. "Unfortunately for you, my so-called teacher is a sick man. His country place is his place of rest. His Right of Privacy as a citizen of adult responsibility` is naturally even stronger, under the circumstances. You won't be able to obtain a warrant to enter his grounds without showing just cause. However, I'd be the last to prevent you from trying."

There was a pause of moderate length, and then Quinn leaned forward, so that his imaged-face expanded and the fine lines on his forehead were visible, "Byerley, why do you carry on? You can't be elected."

"Can't I?"

"Do you think you can? Do you suppose that your failure to make any attempt to disprove the robot charge—when you could easily, by breaking one of the Three Laws—does anything but convince the people that you *are* a robot?"

"All I see so far is that from being a rather vaguely known, but still largely obscure metropolitan lawyer, I have now become a world figure. You're a good publicist."

"But you *are* a robot."

"So it's been said, but not proven."

"It's been proven sufficiently for the electorate."

"Then relax—you've won."

"Goodbye," said Quinn, with his first touch of viciousness, and the visorphone slammed off.

"Good-bye," said Byerley impertubably, to the blank plate.

Byerley brought his "teacher" back the week before election. The air car dropped quickly in an obscure part of the city.

"You'll stay here till after election," Byerley told him. "It would be better to have you out of the way if things take a bad turn."

The hoarse voice that twisted painfully out of John's crooked mouth might have had accents of concern in it. "There's danger of violence?"

"The Fundamentalists threaten it, so I suppose there is, in a theoretical sense. But I really don't expect it. The Fundies have no real power. They're just the continuous irritant factor that might stir up a riot after a while. You don't mind staying here? Please. I won't be myself if I have to worry about you."

"Oh, I'll stay. You still think it will go well?"

"I'm sure of it. No one bothered you at the place?"

"No one. I'm certain."

"And your part went well?"

"Well enough. There'll be no trouble there."

"Then take care of yourself, and watch the televisor tomorrow, John." Byerley pressed the gnarled hand that rested on his.

Lenton's forehead was a furrowed study in suspense. He had the completely unenviable job of being Byerley's campaign manager in a campaign that wasn't a campaign, for a person that refused to reveal his strategy, and refused to accept his manager's.

"You can't!" It was his favorite phrase. It had become his only phrase. "I tell you, Steve, you can't!"

He threw himself in front of the prosecutor, who was spending his time leafing through the typed pages of his speech.

"Put that down, Steve. Look, that mob has been organized by the Fundies. You won't get a hearing. You'll be stoned more likely. Why do you have to make a speech before an audience? What's wrong with a recording, a visual recording?"

"You want me to win the election, don't you?" asked Byerley, mildly.

"Win the election! You're not going to win, Steve. I'm trying to save your life."

"Oh, I'm not in danger."

"He's not in danger. He's not in danger." Lenton made a queer, rasping sound in his throat. "You mean you're getting out on that balcony in front of fifty thousand crazy crackpots and try to talk sense to them—on a balcony like a medieval dictator?"

Byerley consulted his watch. "In about five minutes—as soon as the television lines are free."

Lenton's answering remark was not quite transliterable.

The crowd filled a roped-off area of the city. Trees and houses seemed to grow out of a mass-human foundation. And by ultrawave, the rest of the world watched. It was a purely local election, but it had a world audience just the same. Byerley thought of that and smiled.

But there was nothing to smile at in the crowd itself. There were banners and streamers, ringing every possible change on his supposed robotcy. The hostile attitude rose thickly and tangibly into the atmosphere.

From the start the speech was not successful. It competed against the inchoate mob howl and the rhythmic cries of the Fundie claques that formed mob-islands within the mob. Byerley spoke on, slowly, unemotionally—

Inside, Lenton clutched his hair and groaned—and waited for the blood.

There was a writhing in the front ranks. An angular citizen with popping eyes, and clothes too short for the lank length of his limbs, was pulling to the fore. A policeman dived after him, making slow, struggling passage. Byerley waved the latter off, angrily.

The thin man was directly under the balcony. His words tore unheard against the roar.

Byerley leaned forward. "What do you say? If you have a legitimate question, I'll answer it." He turned to a flanking guard. "Bring that man up here."

There was a tensing in the crowd. Cries of "Quiet" started in various parts of the mob, and rose to a bedlam, then toned down raggedly. The thin man, red-faced and panting, faced Byerley.

Byerley said, "Have you a question?"

The thin man stared, and said in a cracked voice, "Hit me!"

With sudden energy, he thrust out his chin at an angle. "Hit me! You say you're not a robot. Prove it. You can't hit a human, you monster."

There was a queer, flat, dead silence. Byerley's voice punctured it. "I have no reason to hit you."

The thin man was laughing wildly. "You *can't* hit me. You *won't* hit me. You're not a human. You're a monster, a make-believe man."

And Stephen Byerley, tight-lipped, in the face of thousands who watched in person and the millions who watched by screen, drew back his fist and caught the man crackingly upon the chin. The challenger went over backwards in sudden collapse, with nothing on his face, but blank, blank surprise.

Byerley said, "I'm sorry. Take him in and see that he's comfortable. I want to speak to him when I'm through."

And when Dr Calvin, from her reserved space, turned her automobile and drove off, only one reporter had recovered sufficiently from the shock to race after her, and shout an unheard question.

Susan Calvin called over her shoulder, "He's human."

That was enough. The reporter raced away in his own direction.

The rest of the speech might be described as "Spoken but not heard."

Dr Calvin and Stephen Byerley met once again—a week before he took the oath of office as mayor. It was late—past midnight.

Dr Calvin said, "You don't look tired."

The mayor-elect smiled. "I may stay up for a while. Don't tell Quinn."

"I shan't. But that was an interesting story of Quinn's, since you mention him. It's a shame to have spoiled it. I suppose you knew his theory?"

"Parts of it."

"It was highly dramatic. Stephen Byerley was a young lawyer, a powerful speaker, a great idealist—and with a certain flair for biophysics. Are you interested in robotics, Mr Byerley?"

"Only in the legal aspects."

"*This* Stephen Byerley was. But there was an accident. Byerley's wife died; he himself, worse. His legs were gone;

his face was gone; his voice was gone. Part of his mind was—bent. He would not submit to plastic surgery. He retired from the world, legal career gone—only his intelligence, and his hands left. Somehow he could obtain positronic brains, even a complex one, one which had the greatest capacity of forming judgements in ethical problems—which is the highest robotic function so far developed.

"He grew a body about it. Trained it to be everything he would have been and was no longer. He sent it out into the world as Stephen Byerley, remaining behind himself as the old, crippled teacher that no one ever saw—"

"Unfortunately," said the mayor-elect, "I ruined all that by hitting a man. The papers way it was your official verdict on the occasion that I was human."

"How did that happen? Do you mind telling me? It couldn't have been accidental."

"It wasn't entirely. Quinn did most of the work. My men started quietly spreading the fact that I had never hit a man; that I was unable to hit a man; that to fail to do so under provocation would be sure proof that I was a robot. So I arranged for a silly speech in public, with all sorts of publicity overtones, and almost inevitably, some fool fell for it. In its essence, it was what I call a shyster trick. One in which the artificial atmosphere which has been created does all the work. Of course, the emotional effects made my election certain, as intended."

The robopsychologist nodded. "I see you intrude on my field—as every politician must, I suppose. But I'm very sorry it turned out this way. I like robots. I like them considerably better than I do human beings. If a robot can be created capable of being a civil executive, I think he'd make the best one possible. By the Laws of Robotics, he'd be incapable of harming humans, incapable of tyranny, of corruption, of stupidity, of prejudice. And after he had served a decent term, he would leave, even though he were immortal, because it would be impossible for him to hurt humans by letting them know that a robot had ruled them. It would be most ideal."

"Except that a robot might fail due to the inherent

inadequacies of his brain. The positronic brain has never equalled the complexities of the human brain."

"He would have advisers. Not even a human brain is capable of governing without assistance."

Byerley considered Susan Calvin with grave interest. "Why do you smile, Dr Calvin?"

"I smiled because Mr Quinn didn't think of everything."

"You mean there could be more to that story of his."

"Only a little. For the three months before election, this Stephen Byerley that Mr Quinn spoke about, this broken man was in the country for some mysterious reason. He returned in time for that famous speech of yours. And after all, what the old cripple did once, he could do a second time, particularly where the second job is very simple in comparison to the first."

"I don't quite understand."

Dr Calvin rose and smoothed her dress. She was obviously ready to leave. "I mean there is one time when a robot may strike a human being without breaking the First Law. Just one time."

"And when is that?"

Dr Calvin was at the door. She said quietly, "When the human to be struck is merely another robot."

She smiled broadly, her thin face glowing, "Good-bye, Mr Byerley. I hope to vote for you five years from now—for co-ordinator."

Stephen Byerley chuckled. "I must reply that that is a somewhat far-fetched idea."

The door closed behind her.

*   *   *

I stared at her with a sort of horror, "Is that true?"

"All of it," she said.

"And the great Byerley was simply a robot."

"Oh, there's no way of ever finding out. I think he was. But when he decided to die, he had himself atomized, so that there will never be any legal proof—Besides, what difference would it make?"

The Subways of Tazoo

COLIN KAPP

The Corps of Unorthodox Engineers has had many strange jobs, but the one on Tazoo looked like one of their worst problems—at first.

"Lieutenant Van Noon, report to Colonel Belling's office."

"Damn!" Fritz Van Noon glared at the loudspeaker. "Sounds as though Belling's back and on the warpath again."

"Can you wonder?" Jacko Hine helped him out from under the miscellanea of half-assembled pieces. "Let's face it, Fritz, some of our recent projects have come unstuck in a rather spectacular manner."

"True," said Fritz, "but never let it be said that the Unorthodox Engineers have produced a damp squib. Always our results have exceeded our wildest expectations."

"Or Belling's wildest fears," said Jacko morosely.

As Fritz entered the office Colonel Belling half raised himself from his chair in greeting. "Ah, Van Noon! Just the fellow I wanted to see."

"Sir?" asked Fritz suspiciously. Colonel Belling was not a man given to cordiality towards his subordinates.

Belling smiled wolfishly. "I've just returned from the General Staff conference. Since you reinstated the railways up on Cannis even the Old Man has been forced to admit that there may be occasions when unorthodox engineering has its virtues. For my part I felt impelled to point out that I'm trying to run a specialist engineering reserve, and that carrying the can for a complete squad of engineering illegitimates was not strictly within my terms of reference. As I explained, always I get stuck with the one engineer in a thousand who should never have left kindergarten, let alone graduated. The only repository I have for these mechanical misfits is the U.E. squad, where the damage they can do, if not exactly nullified, is at least anticipated."

"Isn't that a little unfair, sir? I mean . . ."

"I know just what you mean, Fritz, and I don't accept it. Engineering is a discipline, but the brand you apply is strictly delinquent. The outcome of the conference was that Colonel Nash, whom I'm beginning to suspect has masochistic tendencies, has volunteered to take the U.E. squad on the Tazoon enterprise."

Fritz considered this for a moment. "Exactly what are they doing on Tazoo, sir?"

"Supporting an archaeological team. Life on Tazoo is now extinct, but evidence tends to show that it once held a civilization as highly developed or more so than our own. In terms of knowledge to be gained it is probably the greatest find that space has ever given to us. It is doubtful if the Tazoons were human or even humanoid, and they became extinct at least two million years ago. Our problem is to pick up the remains of a complex mechanical culture as alien and as old as that and attempt to understand it for what it was."

"I shouldn't have thought that was too difficult, sir."

"No, Fritz, I never supposed you would. That's partly the reason you're going. Your inverted-sideways approach is the nearest thing to an alien technology that we've got. That makes you a specialist."

"Thank you, sir," said Fritz warily. "And the other part of the reason we're going?"

"The climatic conditions on Tazoo are such hell that the average rugged ground-cat has a useful working life of about two weeks. That means the archaeologists can't explore far enough from base to get at the really big finds they are certain exist. Fritz, I want you to provide them with transport to where they'll be most use—and if you don't, you'd better find another engineering reserve to come back to, because if you come back here . . ."

"I know," said Fritz unhappily, "you'll make me wish I'd opted to transfer my retirement pay to Tazoo."

"You know, Fritz," said Colonel Belling, "for a moment

we reached a point of real understanding there. I think I'm going to rather enjoy the thoughts of you and the U.E. squad sweating it out in a hell-spot like Tazoo."

Touchdown on Tazoo. The transfer ferry had no viewports and afforded no opportunity for its passengers to receive a preview of their destination. Even the ground-cat which rendezvoused at the landing site close-coupled its hatches with the ferry's airlock before the transfer of passengers and goods began. In the cabin of the ground-cat, shutters likewise obscured the view and cheated Fritz of his moment of revelation.

"Allow me to introduce myself," said the cabin's occupant. "The name is Philip Nevill. Archaeologist in Charge."

"Van Noon," said Fritz. "Engineer extraordinary—and this is Jacko Hine, one of my staff."

Nevill grinned affably. "Your reputation preceded you, my boy. Frankly, when I heard of you I persuaded Colonel Nash to get you here at any cost. There are things on Tazoo it'll take a very liberal mind indeed to understand."

The ground-cat struggled away from the ferry, its engine coughing in asthmatic complaint.

"So I've heard," said Fritz. "Look, do you mind if I open the shutter for a second? I'd like to know the worst right from the start."

"Help yourself," said Nevill, "but I promise you it's a passion you'll soon lose."

Fritz fought the shutter from the window and peered out for his first glimpse of Tazoo. Heavy cloudbanks filtered the furious sunlight to a brilliant monochromatic red which hurt his eyes and rendered all colours as shades of red or the darkest, sooty black. The terrain itself was nothing but a lumpy, featureless waste as far as the eye could see.

"Satisfied?" asked Nevill.

Fritz dropped the shutter back with a clang and closed his eyes.

"Painful, isn't it?" asked Nevill. "Normal endurance is about forty minutes before red-blindness sets in. Very bad for the eyes, to say nothing of the psychological effects. Incidentally, the ultra-violet radiation for two hours after dawn and two hours before sunset is strong enough to take the skin off you in about three minutes flat."

"Charming!" said Fritz. "And what's it like at midday?"

Nevill raised his eyes to the ceiling. "Ruddy awful!" he said.

At the blare of the ground-cat's horn Nevill opened the shutter again. "There's the base—way over yonder."

Fritz scowled at the blood-red panorama. Perhaps half a kilometre away was the base, like a cluster of cherries half-submerged in a waste of pink icing.

"Underground, eh? A very sensible precaution."

"It isn't underground," said Nevill in a slightly aggrieved tone. "It's a surface installation."

"But I don't see anything but some almighty balls of mud."

"They're standard Knudsen huts with a protective skin on. There's a sandstorm that whips up every night which would sandblast an unprotected Knudsen to a skeleton before dawn. We spray each hut weekly with a highly plasticized poly-polymer which is reasonably abrasive resistant. The plastic traps some of the sand and this materially increases its resistance, but builds up and completely ruins the shape."

Abruptly the engine of the ground-cat coughed and died. Nevill held a rapid exchange over the intercom with the driver.

"Engine's gone," he said finally. "Either the carburettor's etched away or the damn sand has got into the cylinders—or both. Anyway, the cat is a write-off for all practical purposes, so there's nothing for it but to walk—and it's too near evening for that to be funny."

They descended from the cabin, Fritz and Jacko choking quietly in the acrid air which caught at their noses and made their lungs feel raw. Nevill, acclimatized, was surveying the sky anxiously. Above them the swirling cloudbanks, blood-red trailing into purple and black, plunged across the darkening sky so low that Fritz had an

almost compulsive desire to put up his hands to see if he
could touch them. There must have been a high wind
above, for the cloudrace was certainly moving at better
than a hundred kilometres an hour, yet on the ground the
warm humidity was deathly still, as though a sheet of glass
insulated them from the driving turbulence.

Nevill was worried. "Looks like a storm," he said.

"Is that bad?" asked Fritz.

"Only if you're unlucky enough to be out in it. Let's
hope it's a wet storm. They're decidedly uncomfortable,
but not usually fatal if you can get to shelter quickly
enough."

"Why, what happens?"

"Nothing spectacular if you can find shelter from a
hundred kilometre per hour damp sandstorm and if you
happen to have sufficient alkali available to neutralize the
rain on your skin."

"Neutralize the rain?" said Fritz, his voice rising. "What
the blazes is in it?"

"Oh, about five per cent sulphuric acid plus a trace of
hydrogen chloride with a little free ionized chlorine. Stings
like hell, but it's better than a dry storm."

"I'll buy it," Fritz said helplessly. "If a wet sandstorm is
equal to an accelerated metal descaling process, what's a
dry storm equal to?"

By now Nevill was deeply concerned, scanning the
furious cloudrace with worried and experienced eyes. They
were still three hundred metres from the nearest part of the
base, with Jacko and the driver close behind.

"I think you're going to have a practical demonstration
of a dry storm, Fritz. If the smell of ozone becomes
intolerable or if you hear anything like a bee buzzing don't
hesitate—just drop to the ground as fast as you are able. If
you can find a hollow then roll into it, otherwise don't
bother—but whatever you do, be quick."

"A bee buzzing?"

"Air ionization path, the prelude to a lightning bolt.
There's a few mega-megavolts not many metres up in the
cloudrace. It packs a current that can not only char a
man but also fuse him neatly into the sand. The

carbon from the body reduces a great many metal oxides in the ground so that the resultant slag forms a remarkable range of glasses."

"Forget the chemistry," said Fritz hastily. "I never could see myself making a very convincing paperweight."

"Then drop!" said Nevill, suiting action to the words.

They all dropped to the ground. Fritz's nose didn't have time to detect the ozone, virtually paralysed as it was by the existing acridity, but his ears did register the sudden buzz which Nevill had anticipated by a half second. Then the lightning bolt, a blaze of vivid energy a mere thirty metres distant, spat like a column of angry fire rising to the heavens. The noise and the shock-wave of its passing stunned them momentarily. By the time they had collected their wits only a generous patch of fused sand and a choking concentration of ozone marked the spot where the bolt had struck.

"Bad!" said Nevill. "Worst I've seen. It's striking low ground, which means we have no possible cover out here. Best throw away any metal you may have on you and try to crawl back nearer to the cat—but for Pete's sake keep your heads low."

Another bolt of lightning, bigger and nearer than the first, stabbed into the sand behind them like the bursting of a shell, followed by three almost simultaneously in the near vicinity.

Desperately slowly the party crawled back towards the cat, which stood as the pitifully-low high-spot of this particular area of terrain. On all sides of them now the jagged lightning cut into the ground with burning shafts of vicious energy, like the arrows of retribution fired by some crazed electric god. Then a shaft burned down on the cat itself. The fantastic current fused the metal into a white-hot bauble which was ripped open by the expanding air within. Before their horrified eyes the cat sank like a lead toy thrown on to glowing embers, and became a dirty, slag-shot puddle of mixed metal and silicates alloying with the red sand of Tazoo.

Then mercifully it began to rain. Nevill turned his face to the stinging, acrid precipitation and let out a howl of pure relief. A few seconds later they were running like half-blinded madmen through the corrosive waters in the direction of the base camp, heedless now of the cracking lightning which had withdrawn to the edge of the rain belt. They were fortunately within a few steps of the base when the wall of sharp, abrasive sand, whipped to fury by a fantastic driving wind, bore down upon them out of the deep purples of the approaching night.

"Welcome to Tazoo, Lieutenant!" Colonel Nash beckoned him into the office.

Fritz explored the still-smarting skin on his face and hands, and was still painfully aware of the puffiness around his eyes.

"Thank you, Colonel. That was quite an initiation ceremony out there!"

Colonel Nash smiled fleetingly. "Unpremeditated, I assure you, but the weather is part of the reason you're here. A ground-cat is the toughest machine available, but as you saw for yourself it is totally incapable of standing up to the environment. The low pH of the celestial waters conspires with the sand to etch and tear the guts out of any transportation contrivance we've yet imported to Tazoo. When you consider atmospheric chlorine, hydrogen chloride, free sulphuric acid, and ozone, plus high humidity and extreme ultra-violet radiation together with an additional nightly sandblast, you can guess that corrosion prevention is not the least of our troubles."

Fritz shuddered involuntarily.

"I must admit," said Nash, "that I haven't always seen eye to eye with you before on the subject of unorthodox engineering, but if you can solve our transport problem I shall at least be open to persuasion. Certainly no orthodox engineers can give us transport on Tazoo at a cost less than the total budget for the entire enterprise."

"What facilities have we?" asked Fritz.

"On Tazoo—anything you can find. If you need anything shipped out from Terra you'll need a damn good case to get it because of shipping costs. Certainly we can't afford to bring any more vehicles out here. Now it's up to you to delve into your unorthodoxy and come up with something practical."

"How is the Tazoon enterprise going?" asked Fritz.

"Slowly," said Nash, "largely because of the aforementioned transport limitations. Nevill's team have uncovered a lot of architectural monstrosities, but the real prize will come if they can find some of the Tazoon mechanical artifacts. If they do, and if they are one half as weird as the rest of the finds so far, it will require all of your peculiar genius to identify and interpret them. We're expecting to find some very unorthodox engineering from a culture which died before the end of the Pliocene period on Terra."

"What signs are there to indicate that they had a highly scientific culture?" asked Fritz. "Surely the finds so far don't indicate very much."

"The preliminary survey party found signs that the Tazoons had reached both of the Tazoon satellites, and we're reasonably certain that they also reached the next planet sunward in this system and actually established a base there."

"All this sounds highly promising," said Fritz. "But two million years is a long time. Would there be anything left of machines and mechanisms after such a period?"

"Nevill theorizes that to develop a high-level functional civilization the Tazoons must have had some pretty good engineers who would have been making due allowances for the make-up of the Tazoon atmosphere. Furthermore, the moist conditions don't penetrate very far down into the sand, so that the deeper an artifact is buried the greater are its chances of almost infinite survival. Deep exploration at a really promising site should give us a slice of Tazoon civilization in a very resonable state of preservation. We need only one good site to justify the whole Tazoon enterprise."

The next day found Philip Nevill in the Archaeological H.Q., apparently none the worse for his previous day's exposure.

"Hullo, Fritz, my boy! What can we do for you?"

"I hope you can answer a question. Do you know what happened to the Tazoons themselves—I mean, why did they become extinct so swiftly when they had achieved such an apparently high technological level?"

Nevill scowled. "You're equating technology with the ability to manipulate environment and thus ensure a higher survival potential. Well, I'm afraid I can't answer that. Indications are that they abandoned the populated areas *en masse* and migrated towards the equatorial regions. From distribution figures it looks as though the entire population set out for the tropics and were decimated on the way. This suggests they were fleeing from something biologically intolerable which claimed a great number in flight."

"Drastic climatic change?" asked Fritz.

"Climatic, no—environmental, possibly. We looked for evidence of major climatic changes, but there's nothing significant that we can trace. The only thing that is recent, geologically speaking, is the sand."

"The sand?"

"Mm! Probably the result of some ecological imbalance. The major plains appear to have once included prolific forests such as are still to be found in places around the temperate belts. For some reason, drought or fire or blight perhaps, these forests died. The results were typically Terran in their pattern."

"Soil erosion?"

"Yes, and on a catastrophic scale. Once the sand got to work on the unprotected soil nothing thereafter got the chance to germinate. We're still picking up viable seeds from the deep diggings, but all the shallow seeds are either dead or had started growth and been uprooted."

"When did this happen—the erosion?"

"We can't tell with certainty, but it appears to slightly pre-date the extinction of the Tazoons themselves. Whether these two factors are related is something only further research can prove. Does that answer your question?"

"Yes, but only to pose another," said Fritz. "I don't understand how any culture technically able to explore the neighbouring satellites could have been wiped out by anything as foreseeable and reversible as soil erosion. And why migrate to the tropics when the soil fertility remained in the temperate belts?"

"I don't know," said Nevill. "It's a difficult problem. The Tazoons were not even humanoid, and the probability is that neither their physiology nor their logic had anything in common with our own. It could be misleading if we attempted to interpret their actions by simple extrapolation of what we might have done in similar circumstances."

"A good point," said Fritz. "I don't necessarily agree with it, but I'll bear it in mind. Thanks, Philip, you've given me something to think about."

Having established that the U.E. squad was reasonably well quartered, Fritz turned his attention to the transport problem. This brought him back to Jacko who had compiled a transport survey which he presented with as much enthusiasm as if it had been his own death warrant.

"We're in trouble, Fritz. Of the hundred ground-cats originally provided for the enterprise only twenty are still functioning. Two hundred hours operating life on Tazoo reduces a cat to a condition where you couldn't sell it for scrap value. By sorting bits and pieces we could probably reconstruct another five cats, but we can only reckon on a maximum of six thousand operating-cat-hours before we start walking."

Fritz stared disconsolately at a virgin notebook. "What about tractors and heavy equipment?"

"They're not too bad—but only by virtue of the fact that most of them are still in sealed crates. Once they're broken-out there's no reason to suppose they'll last any longer than the cats do. This combination of corrosion and abrasion is something to which I'd not cheerfully expose a clockwork mouse."

"I take your point," said Fritz. "As I see the present requirements it doesn't give us much over a sixty-day transport potential. What protection can we give to the cats to extend their working life?"

"A lot of a vehicle we can plastic coat, as they do with the Knudsens. The engines are a more difficult problem.

Some genius thought of providing them with standard aluminium-alloy turbine housings, and what the Tazoon atmosphere does to the alloy makes my flesh creep. Even the vitreous liners devitrify and release particles of silica into the bearings."

"Don't bother to describe," said Fritz, "what silica does to the bearings. I think we have to face the fact that while we might save most of the cats themselves we aren't going to be able to save many of the engines. We could devise a system of enclosing the engines in an inert atmosphere—but I doubt if we have the facilities here to do a permanent job. We then also need a supply of controlled pH, moisture-free oxygen for the air intake. I think we could produce that by electrolysis, but I doubt if we can handle it in sufficient quantities to be of much value."

"And so on *ad infinitum*," said Jacko ruefully.

Fritz nodded. "Let's try it anyway. I want two cats modified. Plastic spray them everywhere possible, and seal the engine compartment and fill it with a nitrogen and hydrogen mixture of non-ignitable composition. Get our micro-Linde column working for the nitrogen and make an electrolysis plant for the hydrogen. You'll need both the Linde and the electrolytic plant to get enough oxygen for the air supply for the engine intakes, and you'd better dilute the oxygen with any nitrogen you can spare, then adjust the turbines to run on that."

"And what do I keep the oxygen in?" asked Jacko.

"They've a fair supply of the plastic poly-polymer they use for spraying the huts. It shouldn't be beyond our capacity to blow a gasbag from that."

"It all sounds feasible," said Jacko, "But I doubt the capacity of the micro-Linde to give us all the nitrogen we need."

"So do I," said Fritz, "that's why I said to modify two cats only. There's plenty of other things to try, but this is the most obvious, and we've neither time nor the resources to start nitrogen fixation in a big way." He went to the window, opened the shutter, and stared moodily out at the red and featureless wasteland."

"Sand," he said. "Nothing but sand, fine-grained,

abrasive, and all-pervading. What we need, Jacko, is something completely new in the way of transport on Tazoo. I wonder what the Tazoons themselves employed."

Three days later the modification of the cats was in full swing when the telephone rang.
"Van Noon speaking."
"Fritz, Nevill here. I've got some work for you."
"Bring it over," said Fritz. "A little more won't make much difference."
"Right. Be with you in about ten minutes. It's one of these Tazoon mechanisms we've been looking for."
"Now you have me interested," said Fritz. "Exactly what is it?"
"That's what I want you to tell me."
Ten minutes later Nevill arrived and ceremonially knocked out his pipe on the threshold in deference to a large no-smoking notice. Then he signalled to his assistants who dragged a large object into the hut and dropped it on the floor.
Fritz looked at it dubiously.
"I think you've come to the wrong department. It looks like the great-grandaddy of an alien chicken wishbone once belonging to some grandaddy alien chicken. Why not present it to the biology boys?"
"I did," said Nevill, "but they sent it right back with the message that you were responsible for investigating machinery."
"Machinery?" Fritz surveyed the acquisition moodily. "Have you tried it on the catering department? Perhaps they could turn it into some sort of broth."
"Machinery," said Nevill firmly. "And I'll tell you why. It isn't animal, it's vegetable—Tazoon ironwood to be precise. Also, it didn't grow that way. It was manufactured, or at least trimmed to shape, as witness the tooling marks. Further-more, the Tazoons were plenty fond of them because the Southern plain out yonder has them at an estimated density of nearly half a million to the square kilometre."
Fritz choked for a full half minute. "Half a million?"
Nevill noddedd. "And that plain is pretty big. If the

sampling we have done is representative of the whole area there could be something like five thousand million of those on that one plain alone. I know the Tazoons were alien beyond our conception of the word, but I just can't see them producing that many just for the hell of it. That would be an exercise akin to paving the Sahara desert with pencil sharpeners. It's my belief that the wishbones are something functional. I want you to tell me what they were and what their function was."

Fritz nodded. "I'll let you have a preliminary report in a day or so, but if that's a machine I should hate to see their idea of a great big alien chicken wishbone."

After Nevill had left, Fritz spent a quiet hour examining the wishbone from all angles and going all over the surface of it with a magnifying glass looking for clues as to its function. Then Jacko had the wishbone hauled to the work-shop for a more thorough examination. He reported back when the work was completed.

"I think we have something here, Fritz. You know those nodules on the inner surfaces, well, the fluoroscope shows a dark mass of some foreign material in each. If you're agreeable we're proposing to cut one out and see what it is."

"Start cutting," Fritz said, "because if this is a sample of Tazoon engineering then the sooner we start to come to grips with it the better."

Reluctantly the bandsaw cut into the ancient ironwood. Halfway through, the blade screeched complainingly on some hard inclusion. Then the module became detached, and from inside it Jacko shook a large, bright crystal on to the table.

"I thought as much," said Fritz. "There are metal fibres in the structure of the wishbone and metallised facets on the crystal. On this evidence I'd say this was some form of piezo-electric device. And see how the crystal is drilled—do you suppose there could have been strings across the wishbone?"

Jacko counted the nodules equal on both sides. "Lord, a harp!" he said in a voice heavy with incredulity.

"Or a sound-transducer," said Fritz. "There are common electrical paths through the ironwood, and connections to the crystals. If you applied an alternating current to those contacts, the crystals would excite the strings in sympathy according to the resonant frequency of the particular system. I wonder what on earth it would sound like? Jacko, start restringing what's left of this thing while I sort out a power amplifier and a few bits and pieces. Together we can make some be-eautiful music."

"Right," said Jacko, "but if your conception of music is anything like your engineering I'm going to take time out to make some earplugs too."

It took three hours to complete the assembly. Fritz disappeared to the communications hut and returned with an assortment of equipment which he appeared to assemble more by inspiration than by design. When everything was ready, he switched on. The first results were shattering, and the electronics needed drastic revision before a reasonably tolerable result was obtained.

After some final adjustments Fritz pronounced himself satisfied with the results and dropped into a chair to listen attentively, his gaze wandering to the open shutter and the blood-red sunset trailing nakedly beyond.

"Listen to it, Jacko!" said Fritz happily. "Alien and beautiful beyond recall."

"I might just point out," said Jacko, "that if somebody attempted to restring a two-million years old grand piano with stranded cable and without any idea of the scale and pitch involved, the results would sound equally alien."

"I'm in no mood to quibble with one who possesses such a tiny soul," said Fritz. "To me this is music such as the ancient Tazoons knew it as they walked hand in hand in the eyeless evenings of old Tazoo. Can't you imagine it, Jacko, this incredible music voiced by a million harps in the blood-red twilight of this alien land?"

"It makes my head ache," said Jacko. "What are you feeding into the blasted thing, anyway?"

Fritz coughed. "Actually it's the telemetry signals from the satellite monitoring the Tazoon ionosphere, but the harp contributes about five hundred per cent distortion, so you never know it from music."

"I can't help feeling distinctly uneasy," said Jacko, "about the notion of anybody wanting half a million crazy self-playing harps to the square kilometre. No culture could be that fond of music and yet survive."

"They didn't survive. And we can't yet hope to understand so alien a culture. If you want a parallel, think of all the millions of personal transistor radios taken to the beaches on Terra on a public holiday. Think how much simpler life would be if they erected loudspeakers at four-foot intervals on all beaches and made full-time listening compulsory instead of merely unavoidable."

Despite the warmth Jacko shuddered visibly and closed his eyes, while the complex tones of the harp sang strangely with unfathomable harmonies which did curious things to his stomach. "I'm beginning to get the idea," he said, "exactly why the Tazoons decided to migrate. Listening to this, I get precisely the same urge myself."

At that moment the door was flung open and Nevill, eyes aglow with jubilation, burst into the hut.

"Fritz, we've done it! A real find at last. To judge from the extent of our soundings we seem to have hit upon the location of a whole damn Tazoon city under the sand."

Fritz bounded up with enthusiasm. "Congratulations, Philip! This sounds like the breakthrough we've been waiting for. Exactly where is this site?"

"Under our very noses—about twenty kilometres east of here. I tell you, Fritz, my boy, there's a real metropolis down there."

He stopped, aware for the first time of the singing harp.

"What in the name of Thunder is that?"

"A genuine Tazoon harp in action," said Fritz modestly. "Don't you like it?"

"No," said Nevill, "because it isn't right. Nobody, however alien, would want more than one of anything that sounds like that. Besides"—he mopped the moisture which had risen on his brow—"the Tazoons had very small ear cavities. Their audible range was undoubtedly in the medium ultrasonic. Frankly they could never have heard anything pitched as low as that. Sorry! Try and make it do something else like lighting fires or something."

And so saying, he was gone, leaving Fritz looking miserably at his equipment and trying to avoid Jacko's eyes.

"All right," said Fritz, "so even I can't always be right first time." He turned off the amplifier disconsolately. "I still think it was a good idea."

"That's the second of your good ideas that has run off the rails today," said Jacko, fingering his ears.

"Second?" Fritz looked mildly surprised.

"Yes, I forgot to tell you. Your idea for obtaining pure nitrogen for the cats by fractional distillation in the micro-Linde didn't solve the problem, it merely transferred it. The blasted Tazoon atmosphere's eaten the guts out of the Linde compressor."

"That was all I needed to make my day!" said Fritz. "You'd better get the boys together, Jacko. I want every repairable ground-cat and tractor prepared for operation, and as much heavy lifting and moving tackle as we can acquire."

"What are you planning, Fritz?"

"Let's face it, Jacko, we can't keep enough transport in service to do the daily forty-kilometre round-trips to the new site for very long. If that's a major site they've found there won't be much point in having a base camp this far distant. The logical thing to do is expend all our resources, moving the whole base to the new site."

"Are you crazy?" asked Jacko. "It'd take months to dismantle this lot and transport it that far."

"I said nothing about dismantling. A Knudsen hut is a unit structure. It is capable of being moved as a whole. Can you think of any reason why we shouldn't just attach a cat or tractor to each hut and haul it bodily over the sand to the new site?"

"Yes, Colonel Nash and the base psychiatrist, to name only two. A Knudsen could never stand a belting like that and finish in one piece."

"Ordinarily, no, but these have been covered with alternate layers of resin and sand to a thickness which has become ridiculous. Dammit, Jacko, you've got a metal and sand-filled resin laminate there which must have all of a hundred and fifty times the strength of the original hut."

"You're dead right, of course," said Jacko. "But I'm going to love thinking of you trying to explain it to Colonel Nash."

"All right," said Nash at last. "You can start moving the base just as soon as the necessary cables and services have been laid. I don't need to remind you that everything has to be fully secured by sundown. And I warn you that if anything goes wrong . . ."

He leaned back speculatively for a moment.

"You know, Fritz, I must confess I'm disappointed. I'd expected great things from unorthodoxy, but when it comes to the point you can't even promise to keep a decent transport system in operation."

"A snowflake," Fritz protested, "wouldn't stand much chance in Hell unless you had a ton of refrigeration equipment alongside. The fault is not being in Hell, but in being a snowflake. You've got a roughly similar position with your cats on Tazoo. A suitable cat could easily be designed for these conditions, but it would need Terran resources to build it and a long haul to bring it out here. The cost would be astronomical. The limitation is in associating transport with the idea of a ground-cat."

"I'm perfectly aware of that," said Nash. "In fact it's the reason I sent for you. You have the reputation for producing the impossible at very short notice. All right—I challenge you to produce."

"Miracles we perform immediately," said Fritz quietly. "The impossible takes a little longer. After all, we've only been here a week."

Nash watched him narrowly for a moment. "Fritz, frankly I don't believe anybody has the remotest chance of doing what I ask, but I'm calling your bluff. If you have any sort of transport running on Tazoo in three months' time I'll be glad to take back all the harsh things I've ever said about U.E. If you don't I'll have to send you back to Terra. The Tazoon enterprise wasn't designed to carry any dead weight."

"It's a challenge I'll accept," said Fritz, "but don't

expect to equate transportation with any vehicular form
you're used to, because the chances are a million to one
against it looking like anything you've ever seen before."

Jacko was waiting for him outside the office.

"Bad?" he asked.

"Not good," said Fritz. "We've got three months to
crack the transport problem or get kicked out as a bunch of
no-good layabouts. The honour—even the continuance of
U.E.—is very much at stake. Somehow we've got to con-
trive some sort of vehicle, and this in the face of the fact that
we have no source of constructional material capable of
withstanding the Tazoon environment."

"So where do we go from here, Fritz?"

"Damned if I know. You go and check the arrangements
for the big move. I'm going over to the site to see how
friend Nevill is doing. He may have dug up a little
inspiration out there—and Heaven knows I could use a
little right now."

Nevill saw the cat drawing across the rouge desert, and
came to the edge of the workings to await Fritz's arrival.

"How're things going, Philip?"

"Wonderful, my boy. We knew we had a major find, but
this—this is paradise! We're going straight down on a
major city by the look of it, and the stuff on the lower levels
where the sand is dry is in a perfect state of preservation.
Some of the three-storied buildings are so sound that we'll
be able to use them for our own purposes. I tell you, Fritz,
the Tazoon enterprise looks like paying off about two
million per cent interest. The complete analysis of the stuff
found here will occupy generations."

Fritz gazed down into the broad quarry which was the site
of the workings. On every hand the feverish activity of the archaeological teams pointed a measure of the excitement and
enthusiasm which infected everyone concerned. The shifts
had been voluntarily lengthened, but even so, the end of
the shift period had to be declared a compulsory cessation
of work lest those on the trail of such immeasurable archaeological delights should endanger their health by continuing until they dropped from exhaustion.

Here and there alien towers were already exposed above the sand, unimaginable obelisks of incomprehensible architecture, curiously distorted and decayed by time and the ravages of wind and sand. Some, the sand shored back to greater depths, were firmer on the lower levels, and the architecture was even more marvellously and more inconceivably wrought. Occasionally, vertical pits descended at points where logic had decreed there lay something more intriguing or exciting or yielding greater bounty for the effort it entailed.

Fritz was fascinated beyond measure. The clawing other-worldliness drew his imagination on with an inescapable lure. As an engineer he fought to tame the logic of the structures which were being uncovered before him, but something in his soul, poesy perhaps, denied him an identification of parts and trapped him in the wonder of the whole. He was the technologist who came for a dispassionate analysis and stayed to worship.

With great resolve he wrenched his mind from its journeyings and looked at Nevill appealingly. The latter patted him on the soulder sympathetically. "I know, my boy," he said. "It takes us all like that. It's both wonderful and sad to be uncovering the remains of so great a culture: wonderful because the culture was so great, and sad because we find their city empty of the creatures who created it."

"Why the hell did they have to go?" asked Fritz. "After they'd got all this way? They had mastered their environment to a degree comparable to ourselves, then in the space of a few short centuries they faded and died away and the sand moved in and covered all their marvels. But for what reason did they go? It's something we must discover lest it also comes upon us."

By sundown the last hut had been transferred to its new position near the workings. The day had been one of great activity intermixed with frustration. As Fritz had foreseen the huts had proved themselves capable of being moved bodily across the sand, but the condition of the cats and tractors was such that the path of the move was plainly marked with a trail of abandoned vehicles spread broadly across the sandy steppes. Indeed, by the end of the day only five cats remained in operation.

After organizing a team to recover any repairable cats, Jacko went to look for Fritz and found him in the workshop idly strumming the Tazoon harp with the air of a man evoking the muses as an aid to inspiration.

"You know, Jacko, I wish I could work out what happened to the Tazoons. I simply can't understand why such a highly advanced and organized culture should suddenly fall to pieces. There's no suggestion of a major war, and there's not sufficient radioactive material on the planet to make a nuclear holocaust a possibility. It's a highly disturbing thought that a catastrophe which could destroy a race with that level of technology could leave so little trace. It's as though they suddenly closed up their cities and walked out to die on a mass trek to the equator."

"What about famine?" asked Jacko.

"Possibly. That's virtually what Nevill suggested—widespread soil erosion. For some reason the major forests in this zone died suddenly. That rather suggests a prolonged drought—but you'd think a major technology fighting for survival could cope with even that. The sea is an atrocious mineral stew, but I'm willing to bet you could distil enough water to maintain a pretty fair agricultural belt if the need arose."

"But without nuclear energy where would you get that sort of power?" asked Jacko. "Distillation of sea-water on that scale would take a great deal of energy."

"Power!" Fritz sat up. "Now there's an idea! Come to think of it, where did they get their power from anyway? Let's put a few facts together. We know that at a certain stage in the history of Tazoo something happened— something which in the span of a couple of centuries destroyed the civilized inhabitants of the planet. Curiously, the wild-life forms survived for a considerable time afterwards, and some are still to be found in the forest belts. Now the basic difference between civilized and wild-life forms is that the former are power dependent animals while the latter are not. Jacko, my dear fellow, you may have hit upon something there."

"It's just a gift," said Jacko modestly.

"Then seeing it didn't cost you anything, see if you can stretch it a little farther. Let's play for a moment with the assumption that the Tazoons had become power-dependent animals—as we have ourselves. What would their basic source of energy have been if it could have failed suddenly and disastrously?"

"Oil or natural gas, perhaps," said Jacko.

"Not very convincing. By all appearances the Tazoons were great power users. From what Nevill's uncovered recently I'd say the power consumption in this area alone must have been quite fantastic even by Terran standards. Now, you don't develop a heavy power-consuming technology unless you've a good idea that you have the resources to maintain it. To do otherwise would be technological suicide."

"That's assuming they thought about the problem in the same way that a human being would."

"I wouldn't know about human beings," said Fritz drily, "but engineers I do know about, and their thought processes must be essentially similar whether they have one head or six. There are an infinite number of ways of solving any engineering problem, but the simpler answers will always look familiar. It's just the nature of the beast. Give a ten-armed Dingbat a head of steam and tell him to convert it into electrical energy. I don't care what the influence of his racial characteristics, training, or personal geometry, somewhere, at some point, he's going to fall into a chain of logic familiar to engineers of similar calibre anywhere. Ergo, I don't think we can go far wrong if we tackle this problem from our own standpoint, and currently we are assuming they had a power supply which appeared infallible yet failed. Now we need to know what was the source of that energy. If we knew that maybe we could work out why it stopped."

The telephone rang and Fritz answered it. Nevill had been searching for him.

"Fritz, I'd like to see you first thing in the morning. There's something I want you to take a look at."

"Right! Something promising?"

"I imagine so. The team has just uncovered something which looks like the entrance to a mine of some sort. Perhaps you'd like to look it over."

"We'll be there first thing," said Fritz.

"What's up?" asked Jacko.

"Nevill's team have discovered what he thinks may be the entrance to a mine."

"In the centre of a city?"

"The same question occurred to me," said Fritz. "I don't think that a mine is particularly probable, though it might just be connected with our lost energy source—or he may have stumbled on something I've been looking for myself."

"What's that?"

"Jacko, in a city as large and as complex as this one appears to be, where's the logical place to put the bulk passenger transport system?"

"Underground," said Jacko, "same as always."

"Precisely, and that's what I'm hoping Nevill's hit upon."

"God!" said Jacko. "An alien subway scarcely bears thinking about."

Further in from the door they had to use flashlights. Here the sand had not penetrated so deeply, and by the time they had reached the head of the shaft only a brief dusting covered the floor.

The shaft was equipped with the normal Tazoon-type stairway—a central pole with round horizontal bars set in a helix, but on a broader pattern than they had encountered hitherto and with a deeper pitch. Such a stairway was not adapted to humans, but it was traversable by those with climbing experience or suicidal tendencies. Jacko had neither.

"Down?" he inquired, his flashlight failing to probe the darkness of the alien depths.

"Down," said Fritz. "Where's your sense of adventure?"

"It remained firmly embedded in my childhood," said Jacko, "along with the sense necessary not to get into situations like this."

"Down!" said Fritz firmly, and suited actions to his words.

Together they climbed down perhaps one hundred metres. Since it was impossible both to climb and hold a flashlight, this was accomplished in total darkness, and the steady rhythm of the climb from bar to bar exercised its own almost hypnotic fascination. Both had to stand for many seconds at the bottom to reorientate their senses.

The preservation of the passageways at that level was remarkable and probably complete, and the air was cooler and less aggressive than above. Remarkable also was the dryness of the connecting tunnels which had lain for so long at such a depth, indicating the complete lack of a water table above the level of the deep-welled seas of Tazoo. The walls here were of metal, curiously wrought in a manner which might have been functional or might have been symbolic; and the alien strangeness of a completely artificial Tazoon environment gripped at their hearts with a half fear which had nothing to do with self-preservation. For the first time they felt the full impact of standing in the presence of the logical but unimaginable achievements of a culture which had no common roots with their own. They could vaguely comprehend but never predict the unfolding of the unearthly technology which surrounded them.

Machines or effigies, they had no means of knowing which, stood like dark, mute sentries in the uncertain, shifting shadows of the flashlamp's beam: the tortuous walls and fluted ceilings were channelled and moulded with a thousand metal mouths connected to unguessable throats for unfathomable reasons—only the floor approximated its Terran counterpart, having a common engineering function of providing an unimpeded pedestrian passageway.

They turned another corner and stopped abruptly when the flashlamps' beams soared into empty darkness and encountered nothing. Their consternation was relieved by the realization that they were now looking along the length of a vastly greater tunnel than any they had so far traversed. Vaguely they could trace the complex vaulted roof rising to its apex in a series of panels shaped to some intriguing algebraic equation. At their feet the floor continued unchanged as far as the flash-beams could reveal, while to their right the level dropped abruptly perhaps two metres to form a channel of about seven metres width. Beyond the channel rose the walls again arching upwards.

"Are you thinking what I'm thinking?" asked Fritz.

"Uh!" said Jacko. "No matter how you build it, a subway station is a subway station is a subway station, and this is just one such."

"Good man," said Fritz. "I want to have a look at the rails."

Together they surveyed the channel, probing minutely with their flashlights.

"No lines," said Jacko at last, his voice tinged with dissapointment. "It could be that we're wrong about this place. Perhaps a sewer..."

"I'm not wrong," said Fritz. "I'd know a subway when I found one even if I was deaf, blind, and shut up in a box. It's part of the chemistry of whatever genes conspire to make an engineer. Here, help me down, I want to explore."

"Don't you think we'd better go back and get some reinforcements?" said Jacko. Fritz had started along the channel to where it entered a somewhat smaller tunnel undeniably reminiscent of a Terran subway. "For Heaven's sake, Fritz, you don't know what you might find in there!"

"What's eating you, Jacko? Not losing your nerve all of a sudden?"

"No, it's just that walking down a tunnel that *might* contain an emergent subway train goes against my finer sensibilities—even if it is two million years behind schedule."

Fritz took fifteen paces into the tunnel and let out a whoop which paralyzed Jacko with fright.

"Jacko, get down here quick! I've found one."

"Found one what?" asked Jacko when he had regained control of his vocal cords.

"A train, you idiot. I've found a blessed train! Fetch the other lamp."

Against his better judgment Jacko dropped into the

channel and followed Fritz into the tunnel. Then with a churning stomach and racing brain he examined the artifact which barred their further entry.

"That," he asked finally, "is a train?"

"It can't be anything else," said Fritz, not very happily. "It doesn't appear to be a signal box and there's not much point in having a wrought-iron summer house this far underground. It appears to be the right shape to fit the tunnel so it's probably either a highly ornate tunnelling machine or else it's a train."

"Alien!" said Jacko in awe. "The connotations of that word get lost by common usage. It doesn't begin to convey the mind-twisting sense that everything you know and believe has been scrunched up and re-sorted by a different kind of logic. These people had different values and different basics, and it makes the mind squirm even trying to readjust."

"They didn't have different basics," said Fritz, "they merely had a different emphasis on the relative values of the same old basics. We can't yet try to comprehend the culture, but when it comes to unravelling their engineering I think we shall find we have a great deal in common."

"Like an iron-lace potting-shed without wheels or tracks which we presume to be a train simply because it doesn't appear to be anything else?"

"Just so," said Fritz. "We have to separate the mechanics from the culture. As far as we've gone we've found very few Tazoon applications of principles of which we were completely ignorant. Of course, they were streets ahead of us in some fields and curiously lacking in others—they had no organic chemistry, for instance. But they don't appear to have dabbled in the occult, so if that's a train it's only a matter of time before we find out what made it go."

Cautiously they squeezed down between the curious vehicle and the tunnel wall, the better to examine the structure's complexity and strangeness.

"It's a crazy, twisted birdcage," said Jacko finally. "An appliance for containing crazy, twisted birds."

Fritz looked up from the complex of curiously wrought

mechanisms. "We'd better get some more lights down here, and muster some of the squad. I want this insane dumpling-container taken to pieces and put together again when I've had a chance to examine the pieces."

"Cannibalization I can understand," said Jacko, "But why the resurrection?"

"Because," said Fritz Van Noon, "if it's the last thing I do I'm going to put the subways of Tazoo back in operation. We obviously can't build a transportation system on the surface, but here we have a ready-made nucleus which already goes halfway to meet the problem."

"I demand to be invalided out of the Service on the grounds of insanity," said Jacko, "your insanity. I thought we'd had enough of railways up on Cannis."

"That was different," said Fritz. "There we were merely up against physical obstacles such as errant volcanoes. This is specifically an exercise in matching technologies. All we have to do is to determine which part of the railway system moves and which part is intended to stay still. That shouldn't be too difficult, now should it?"

"Not when reduced to such basic terms," Jacko agreed dourly. "But I know you. You never realize when you're beaten."

"I've told you before," said Fritz sternly, "there's no such thing as a physical impossibility. A limitation is a state of mind, not a question of fact. Here we are faced with the work of an alien race with a technological and scientific level roughly comparable to our own. Providing we hold that one fact paramount we ought to be able to unscramble any device this planet has to offer—and make it function for our own service if we wish."

"Providing one thing holds good," said Jacko. "We have first to be able to recognise a thing for what it is. It's no good dismantling a Tazoon milk-strainer if we're under the impression that it ought to be a transistor superhet—or *vice-versa,* come to think of it."

Fritz reported back to Philip Nevill. The latter listened to the details of the find with the air of suppressed jubilation which was rapidly becoming his permanent expression.

I

Then he ran his fingers through his untidy hair and searched for his pipe with a distracted grin.

"Fritz, my boy, this is perfectly marvellous. What a day we've had! We've opened up so many promising new lines of research that the whole damned thing is getting out of hand. We could do with five hundred trained archaeologists to digest the meat in this lot, and even then we couldn't do more than scratch the surface. The impact of building techniques alone on Terra is going to be fantastic, and when the whole complex is assembled into Terran know-how its impact on the human race will be so great that our own culture will never be quite the same again.

"If you really want to make your mark on the enterprise, then take over this subway completely, because I shan't be able to get round to it for five years at least. Do a complete technical run-down on it, as detailed as you like. Do anything you like with it which won't impair its archaeological value. All I ask is a comprehensive progress report in time for each data shipment to Terra."

"Fair enough!" said Fritz. "I want to open up the buildings directly above the station to look for ancillaries."

Nevill glanced at his sketch map and drew a line through two diagrammatical blocks. "It's all yours," he said, "but don't drive yourself daft trying to comprehend too much too fast. You'll find you have to absorb Tazoon environments rather than understand them. Sooner or later the pieces fit themselves into place. And Heaven knows there's enough pieces available for fitting—a jigsaw embracing the life and work of a complete culture."

"We've just got ourselves a subway," said Fritz, as he rejoined Jacko at the workings. "We're going to open up the building here and see what's inside."

"Who's we?" asked Jacko suspiciously.

"You," said Fritz. "I'm going below again to see if I can trace any control sequence running up from below. I want you to go in there and see if you can find anything similar running down. We'll meet at the end of the shift and compare notes. You know what to look for—cable groupings or anything which suggests that it might have a control or power function."

"You're really set on this, aren't you?" Jacko said. "About using it, I mean."

"Certainly," said Fritz. "Let's face it, if Fritz Van Noon can't restart an alien subway, then who in the universe would you expect to be able to do it?"

"I was afraid you'd ask that," said Jacko.

An hour later they met again at the portals of the building.

"There's a sort of power and control complex which appears to come down somewhere near the farther end here," said Fritz.

Jacko nodded. "I picked up the end of that," he said. "There's a channel running through the basement of the building, and the complex rises into that, and is then split into sections which are fed to the floors above."

"What's it like in there?" asked Fritz.

"Weird," said Jacko. "There's no other word to describe it. It's like the epitaph to an insane, overgrown spider with a compulsive spite against inverted single-head broaching presses."

"Thank you," said Fritz. "I can imagine it all too clearly."

Jacko's description of the basement of the building was, if anything, an understatement. The ground floor proved inconceivably worse, and the situation deteriorated rapidly as they ascended to the higher floors. The subway had possessed the crude simplicity of a functional unit, but the detail and complexity of the levels in the building above defied analysis or description. For a long time no object which they examined provided any sort of clue as to its function, and they traversed the cluttered levels with an increasing sense of dismay and frustration. As with most of the larger buildings only the top storeys had suffered any considerable decay, and the sand and damp had not penetrated into the interiors to any great extent, so that the state of preservation on the levels in which they were interested was excellent.

Fritz's spirits were nearing their lowest ebb as he battled with an ocean of incomprehensibilities, until he entered the final gallery. Here he stopped, groping for form in the alien pattern, then seized a glimpse of illuminated understanding and fanned it into a flame.

"Jacko! Do you know what this is? Don't you see—electrical control gear."

Jacko was unimpressed. "If this is their idea of electrical control gear I should hate to see their version of a collection of crazy, twisted maypoles."

"It doesn't matter," said Fritz. "The approach may be alien, but the underlying logic is inescapable. Unless I miss my guess this is an automatic switching system, and from its complexity I should think it's pretty comprehensive. It may even be the only switching system for the whole of the Tazoon subways. You realise what that means?"

"About fifteen years' circuit analysis," said Jacko morosely.

"No. Look at the condition of this stuff. The preservation is as good here as it is in the subway itself. The chances are it's still functional. We'd only have to reconnect the power to get the whole thing back into operation."

"Perish the thought!" said Jacko. "I may be a bit naïve, but assuming—just for the sake of argument—that what we've found is a subway, where would you get the energy to power it? Subways need a lot of power, and if the Tazoons ran out of it how are you going to find it?"

"We'll worry about that later. It may not be easy, but I have one advantage the Tazoons didn't have—access to the complete technologies and resources of a scientific culture which was completely alien to the Tazoons. I don't doubt that Colonel Nash could be persuaded to bring an MHD oscillating-plasma generator out from Terra, but that's a last resort. As an unorthodox engineer I'd prefer to locate the original Tazoon power source and see if a completely fresh engineering approach could start it producing again."

"So what's the plan?" asked Jacko.

"Get Harris and a couple of the electrical boys to join me here to try and analyse the circuit logic. Meanwhile you take the rest of the squad below and start dismantling the train. Between us we should discover enough about the

way the Tazoons handled electricity and mechanisms to
have a fair idea of how to make these pieces work."

"You think so?" asked Jacko. "I still haven't forgotten
what you did to that ruddy harp."

Fritz's team did indeed manage to establish a certain
amount of circuit logic, and once a few principles were
known the work progressed rapidly. They concentrated
mainly on the huge switching columns, swiftly realizing
that what at first sight could be mistaken for relative
crudity was in fact an ingenious and sophisticated short-cut
technique to solve a highly complex sequence-switching
problem. Among other things they discovered that the
assembly was probably built to handle alternating current
with an efficiency peaking at about ten kilocycles a second,
although such periodicity seemed unlikely in practice. The
current handling capacity of the assembly was staggeringly
high. Breakdown voltages too were high, but afforded no
real clues as to the normal operating potentials. Safety
precautions against unshielded conductors were non-
existent, and they were forced to the conclusion that either
the equipment was designed to operate unattended or else
the physiology of the Tazoons had rendered them immune
to electric shocks which would be lethal to their Terran
counterparts. The apparatus which logically should have
been metering equipment, however, made no sense at all.

Somebody was soon at work rigging up a communicator
to connect the switching gallery with the subway. When
the line was functional Jacko was the first to make a call.

"Fritz we've run into a snag on this train dismantling
project. We can't get the blasted thing apart. Tell me I'm
crazy if you like, but I'd swear the train was cast as a whole
and not fabricated—moving parts included."

"Cast in a pattern of that complexity in steel?" asked
Fritz incredulously.

"Not steel," said Jacko. "Titanium, unless I judge my
metals wrong."

"That only makes it worse," said Fritz. "Come to think
of it, we were being a bit naïve expecting a two-million-year
extinct culture to leave something which could be

dismantled with a hammer and a pair of Stillsons. Is there no hope at all?"

"We could take an atomic-hydrogen torch or a cutting laser and chop it into two-inch slices, but I doubt if Nevill would react favourably to the idea."

"Come to think of it," said Fritz, "neither would I. Better abandon the project, Jacko, and come back up here. I think I've got a better idea anyway."

"What are you planning now, Fritz?"

"I'm looking at it this way: there are two ways of making a piece of equipment yield the secret of its function—you can dismantle it and worry the principle out of its components, or you can simply set it operating."

"I hope I'm misunderstanding you," said Jacko. "For one ghastly moment I had the idea you were proposing to restart the Tazoon subway without knowing how it worked."

"I was proposing just that. Can you think of a faster way of finding out how it works than by seeing it in action?"

"Is one allowed to resign from the project?" asked Jacko. "Or is suicide the only logical form of escape?"

"You can also be beaten to death by your superior officer, if you're really smitten with an escapist death-wish. We think we've unscrambled the power lines in the gallery here and we've made a guess at what should prove to be the main input lines."

"So?"

"So I want to trace them back to source. Then we can start investigating whether or not we can re-start the native power-producing plant. I want every man I can get employed on tracing those lines, Jacko, and I want you to supervise personally. Remember, we have to get the whole thing operational inside three months if we're to beat Nash's deadline."

"I still think it's a waste of time," said Jacko. "If we're right that the Tazoon civilization collapsed because of lack of power, what chance have we of finding it some two million years later?"

"I suspect the answer is quantitative," said Fritz. "They were trying to run a civilization, we're trying only to run a subway. I'd estimate our requirements at perhaps one ten-millionth of theirs or less. Viewed in that light it doesn't seem too difficult a task, now does it?"

Nevill's team had concentrated on clearing only the tops of the taller buildings. Generally the sand penetration into the interiors was not total, and thus they had access to large modules of Tazoon architectural environment without having to wait for the total clearance which ultimately would follow as resources became available. Once gaining the interior of a building they were relatively free to explore the entire contents of the lower levels. Archaeologically the finds were so incredibly lush that complete classification and analysis would take many decades, and the method therefore used was to set up specialist study groups to make a complete analysis of certain typical areas as a guide to rapidly separating the unique from the mundane when new areas were opened up. Representative samples were carefully crated for transport to Terra, where a more exhaustive examination would be undertaken.

For the next two weeks Fritz himself was kept fully employed in his role as authority on alien science and technology, and the sheer mass of work confronting him could have kept him comfortably occupied for several lifetimes at least. It was now painfully obvious that the staff of the Tazoon enterprise could have been increased a hundredfold and still the finds would have been more numerous than the researchers. Fritz's own work in the field was hampered by the fact that he was working without assistance, the entire complement of the U.E. squad being devoted to locating the elusive power source from which the Tazoons had derived their supply.

On this latter point even Nevill had been unable to offer any help. Although detailed maps of the sectors of the buried city were beginning to be built up there was nothing in them which suggested any power generation or distribution facilities. This was not conclusive, because in very few areas had it yet been possible to excavate below the level of the basic terrain on which the city had been built, and what lay underneath was still a subject for conjecture, but the pattern of conductors disappearing into the depths was sufficient to convince Fritz that whatever the source it was probably not located within the city confines. Jacko's report did not appear to illuminate the situation.

"I tell you, Fritz, that main power input cable you gave us was nothing of the sort. For fifteen blasted days we've traced that thing. A cable it may be, but it's a distribution circuit if it's anything at all."

Fritz scowled. "Are you sure you didn't lose it and pick up another cable in error?"

"Do me a favour!" said Jacko. "We were feeding a signal into the thing at the switching house and picking it up all the way down the cable. I tell you that thing is a distribution complex originating, not terminating, at the subway building."

Fritz sat up sharply. "Distributing power where?"

"I hate to tell you this, but it covers a fair proportion of the Southern plain. The cable divides and subdivides *ad infinitum* as far as we can tell. We counted divisions into roughly forty thousand pairs and that still left a fair majority—but we gave up when we found what was at the end of a dozen or so of the minor pairs. I'll give you three guesses . . ."

"Don't tell me," said Fritz. "I can imagine . . . ruddy great Tazoon harps."

"Harps, harps, and nothing but harps, and never a string between them. Listening to music I could understand, but can you seriously maintain that they installed five thousand million loudspeakers across the plain just so that they could listen to the trains? Nobody could be *that* alien!"

Fritz thumped the table. "Jacko, you're a ruddy genius!"

"Am I?" Jacko blinked.

"Yes. You've given me the clue I needed. Get the squad together, Jacko, we're going to restart the subways of Tazoo."

Ten weeks of the precious three months of Colonel Nash's ultimatum had elapsed before they were in a position to make the preliminary tests. The intervening period had been one of furious activity for the U.E. personnel, and one

over which Fritz had draped a veil of secrecy such that
nobody outside of his group had any idea of the direction
of his slowly unfolding plans. But on the final evening
everything was ready. Fresh cables of Terran newness
threaded their way out of the subway entrance; and on the
platform two dozen floodlights illuminated the mechanical
achievements of a culture which had passed two million
years before, and shone into the tunnel to light a vehicle
which had stopped in that position at the same time that, on
Terra, elephants were native to the Sussex Downs and the
evolving ancestors of man had yet to distinguish
themselves from their animal counterparts.

Shortly before sunset Fritz and his team assembled at the
subway building. Already the calm stasis of the day was
beginning to tremble with unease as the riding cloudrace
overhead broke lower, heralding the nightly windy torment
of the land. This was no lull before the storm but an
increasing tension, a tight coil being further tightened to
the inevitable breaking point which was the lash of the
sandfilled gale. As the storm broke they hastened inside.

Fritz found himself more than slightly in awe of the
thing he contemplated doing. Immaculate as was the
preservation of these Tazoon artifacts he could not help
remembering, as an engineer, the patterns of low
temperature crept, the grain growth, the diffusion—all the
degradation of properties which fabricated metals might be
heir to after two million years of rest. Fortunately the
Tazoons had understood their materials and their
atmosphere well, and apparently had built to last, with a
success which was phenomenal.

In any case, Fritz was now committed. Sentiment and
curiosity apart, the very continuance of the U.E.
depended on his ability to reactivate the subway. He could
not draw back now even though the whole place threatened
to crumble about his head in a welter of dust and thunder.

As was his custom when there were unavoidable risks to
be taken, Fritz alone attended the array of instruments set
up in the subway proper. Jacko was in the switching gallery
on the other end of the communicator, in a hastily
conceived control set-up which included the rest of the

relevant monitoring instruments they had been able to piece together from the inadequate supplies brought to Tazoo, Jacko, uncomfortably aware of the danger of Fritz's position, had sought to dissuade his superior from being present for the actual test run, but Fritz, foreseeing the cataclysmic damage to the installation which might result from the experiment, had decided to be present to gain first-hand experience of the principles of operation which might by their own employment become hopelessly obscured.

Five minutes to zero hour, and Fritz took a last check on his instruments. He had already signalled Jacko to begin preliminary switching when he heard footsteps and voices echoing in the corridors leading to the platform. He snatched up the communicator.

"Hold it, Jacko. I think I've got company. Do nothing until you hear from me."

"Right," said Jacko. "But it's none of our boys down there, I promise you."

"No," said Fritz, "but unless I mistake the gruff undertones it's Colonel Nash and his aides. I'll have to get rid of them, of course. We'd get ourselves a bad name if we knocked off all of the top brass in one go." He slammed down the handset and marched up the platform just as Nash and his retinue arrived.

"Lieutenant Van Noon," said Nash icily, "I have just been informed of your intention of trying to restart the Tazoon subway this evening. As this is a project of the first magnitude I think I should have been more directly informed."

"You will be, sir, as soon as we have anything to report."

"I don't think you quite appreciate my point," said Nash. "If you succeed in this it will be the very first Tazoon mechanical artifact of any moment to have been restarted. As such it is a rather—er—historical occasion. Naturally I'd have liked to have been asked to be present."

"And I don't think you quite appreciate my point," said Fritz. "There comes a point in the progress of any project which is usually obscured by a notice reading: *Danger, Engineers Testing*. As far as we know the Tazoon subway is intact and perfectly preserved. From an engineering point of view there is no reason why we can't switch on the current and have it back in operation as it last was two million years ago."

"Well?" asked Nash ominously. "What's the problem then?"

"Just this," said Fritz. "How do we know that what was normal for the Tazoons is even remotely tolerable for us? The power input for this one sector of the line is quite fantastic by Terran standards. The Tazoons don't appear to have been fools about the efficiency of power conversion, so I can only conclude that Tazoon subway operation was a pretty hectic procedure. When they throw the master switch upstairs we shall have a sample of Tazoon mechanical environment in the raw. I don't want anybody down here at that moment who isn't absolutely essential to the success of the operation."

Colonel Nash snorted with irritation. "The best available information to date indicates that the Tazoons were small-boned, avian, and somewhat fragile creatures. I am perfectly certain that officers of the Terran Exploratory task force are able to tolerate the conditions in a deserted subway every bit as well as its former occupants. But if you happen to be so unsure of your mechanical aptitude why don't you switch things on a piece at a time?"

"Because," said Fritz, "as far as we can tell the whole system is interlocked back to a master computing house of such complexity that it will take all of ten years to unravel the individual controls. For reasons best known to themselves the Tazoons did not appear to have been in favour of local circuit isolators, so we have to accept the whole or nothing at all. I'm making a formal request, sir, for you to leave. If you remain I can't be responsible for the consequences."

"Are you staying, Lieutenant?"

"Yes, sir."

"Then we stay too. I appreciate it's your show, but I think you're overstressing the danger angle."

"Very well," said Fritz. "But remember it was your decision." He returned wearily to his communication point. "Jacko, prepare to switch on."

"Have they gone?"

"No, they insist on staying to see the fireworks."

"Ouch! I hope you know what you're doing."

"If I did," said Fritz, "the chances are that there's nothing on Tazoo which could persuade me to stay on this platform while you throw that switch. Bring the current up to a maximum over thirty seconds and hold it there for three minutes. If you can't contact me on the communicator immediately you've switched off again then get down here fast with all the emergency equipment you've got."

"Right," said Jacko. "And good luck! I'm giving you a count-down of ten . . ."

If Fritz Van Noon was prepared for the worst experience of his life he was still unprepared for the sheer intensity and quality of the impressions which assaulted him. The whole tunnel cavity lit up in a kaleidoscope of lights of unbelievable colour-range and brilliance. The air grew rapidly and uncomfortably hot and choking with acrid vapours which his lungs could not accept and which burned his skin like the breath of a playful blowlamp.

But it was the noise that dug furrows in his soul. A series of rising screams from a dozen mechanical throats passed up through the audible range and into the low ultrasonic, causing dust fires to break out at intervals along the platform. Devices hammered and clattered and chattered in a cacophony which clawed at his eardrums with red-hot needles. Literally every fragment of the installation vibrated or resonated or contributed in some way to the atmosphere of screaming, explosive thunder. Ominously, the train which Fritz had stationed himself to watch, held motionless for a full minute then discharged itself in a rumbling, grinding ricochet into the station and down the farther tunnel, accompanied by a cataclysmic roar which contained all the acoustic qualities of a continuous collision with an unending series of cheap tin tea-trays.

Scarcely had the first train disappeared from view than another skeleton juggernaut hurled itself upon the station and drove a hectic and furious path straight down the line and was gone before his senses could properly interpret its arrival. Fritz cringed before the shock-wave of its passing and watched his precious monitoring instruments scatter in all directions. He ground his teeth in mental pain at the sound of the mechanical anguish of tortured metal biting into tortured metal. Sparks and white-hot fragments showered the platform and peppered his coverall with a pattern of small singed holes.

Colonel Nash and his entourage were now crouched against the wall farther down the platform, white-faced and with their hands over their ears, while some noise-making instrument above aimed horrific noises at their heads. Under their feet the dust smouldered with a repulsive miasmatic odour, reminiscent of kakodyle and mercaptan, which had to be smelled to be believed.

Before Fritz had time to realize the smile that blossomed in his bosom yet another train entered the station, this one fighting to halt itself with a spine-chilling screech of unseen brakes which fought valiantly to kill the horrible momentum. Fritz gritted his teeth and watched its progress right to the last shuddering halt. With his monitoring equipment out of action he was forced to estimate the vehicle's speed mentally and make a rough guess at the forces which would act on the passengers of a vehicle involved in such a drastic reduction of speed. The answer told him more about the physiology of the Tazoons than Nevill had deduced in the previous twelve months.

Abruptly the power died and his eyes were forced to adapt to the relative dimness of the Terran floodlights. His ears still whistled and ached from their recent battering, and the intolerable heat and humidity made him feel like the occupant of some outlandish Turkish bath. Colonel Nash climbed unsteadily to his feet, a perfectly unreadable expression on his face, and picked his way carefully around the heaps of smouldering dust on the platform. His aides, lacking his aplomb, openly betrayed their relief at the end of the ordeal and hastened to the exit.

Nash made straight for Fritz.

"Van Noon."

"Sir?" Fritz saluted briefly while trying to balance a precious audio-frequency spectrum analyser which was in danger of falling off the platform into the channel.

"I owe you an apology," said Nash. "Lord, that was ruddy awful! But you've given me grounds for thought. I'm not saying you didn't warn me—but where in hell did you get all that power?"

"I'll be reporting on that, sir, as soon as I've tidied a few details."

"Very well," said Nash. "There'll be a Staff conference at three o'clock tomorrow in my office. I'd appreciate your answer then."

He turned and strode off, while Fritz became aware of the communicator buzzing urgently.

"Fritz, are you all right?"

"Only just," said Fritz. "It was grim. Everything was at least five times as fast as its Terrain counterpart and about twenty times as noisy, to say nothing of the heat. If that's a sample of a deserted Tazoon subway in operation I hope I never have to suffer one during the rush hour."

"I've got news for you," said Jacko. "We had switching trouble up here on the temporary lines we rigged. According to our calculations we were only able to supply forty-three per cent of the total estimated loading. If you'll hang on for a moment I'll give you a test run at a hundred per cent loading."

"Don't bother," said Fritz hastily. "For that I'd need some repeaters and telemetry equipment plus a few unattended TV cameras. I'm not staying here for a hundred per cent loading run."

"Did you discover anything?"

"Enough. Initially the potential weakness of this system will be confined mainly to its passengers. The Tazoons were apparently using an adaptation of an A.C. linear motor for traction, with the bottom of the channel as the reactive element. On the same principle they use A.C. magnetic flux repulsion to lift the train clear of the ground so that they're virtually hovering on a magnetic flux field. I suspect the same principle should be operating on each side to centre the train with respect to the tunnel walls, only we didn't have enough current to make it fully effective. Come to think of it, it's a damn clever idea, with the train held in a mechanically frictionless supporting field with only inertia, air-resistance, and eddy-current losses to be overcome by the traction system. I can't yet see how the current pickup is arranged, but that's probably inductive too. Suffice it to say we can soon adapt it to our own purposes."

"Good," said Jacko, "only I can't see that by so doing we're going to produce what we set out to achieve. They asked for a transport system and we're offering a subway with all that connotes in the way of limited routes and limited points of access. How long do you think that is going to satisfy Nevill?"

"For at least a lifetime, I should think," said Fritz. "The building of a subway is a climactic achievement in the history of any culture, requiring, as it does, the co-ordination of a considerable quantity of technological resources. Ergo: you only build subways to connect points which are sufficiently important to warrant such endeavour. Give Nevill a functional subway under this city and he will have immediate and convenient access to all those points of the city which the Tazoons themselves thought worth while making accessible. You not only have a transport system but a considerable pointer to the psychology and cultural habits of the Tazoons themselves."

When Fritz arrived at the Staff conference he had the feeling that the rest of the meeting must have been convened about an hour earlier, for the assembly was already engaged in earnest discussion. Nevill was leafing forlornly through a formidable pile of notes, reading abstracts, and Colonel Nash was in the chair.

"Ah, Lieutenant, take a seat. We hope you are going to tell us how you came by that impressive source of energy which enabled you to put on that display last evening in the subway."

"I can do more than that," said Fritz. "I think I can add considerably to our knowledge of the Tazoons themselves. But let us start with the harps—Tazoon harps. I suddenly realised what they were."

"And what was that?"

"Mechano-electric energy converters—piezo-electric generators, if you like. The harps are merely assemblies of high-efficiency piezo-electric crystals operated by the vibrating strings of the harp. The strings are made to vibrate by the passage of the Tazoon night winds."

"I'm no scientist," said Nash, "but I would have thought that piezo-electric effects were scarcely of sufficient magnitude to be useful for energy conversion on that scale."

"A common misconception," said Fritz. "Even our relatively undeveloped Terran ferro-electric ceramics are capable of something better than a power generating density of sixteen watts per square centimetre, which has solar cells beaten hollow. The Tazoon crystals are capable of an output of eighty watts per square centimetre and a conversion efficiency of better than ninety-five per cent, an efficiency markedly better than even the most advanced Terran M.H.D. oscillating-plasma reactors. Mechano-electric conversion has always been a highly promising line of development, but hampered by the fact that on Terra there was a scarcity of large-scale sources of mechanical energy of useful frequency. The Tazoons made ultra large scale use of medium-level energy by utilizing the winds to activate the harp strings. A Tazoon harp in a typical night wind is capable of an output approaching two kilowats. This comes out to around a megawatt of power for each square kilometre of plain equipped with harps."

"Are you sure of this, Fritz?" asked Nevill.

"Perfectly sure. We powered the subway by restringing some of the harps out on the plains there."

"But doesn't the output vary with the force of the wind?"

"Yes, but with the harps ranged over a wide area the variations average out fairly well."

"But how did they obtain their power when there was no wind?"

"They didn't," said Fritz. "We've found nothing which would indicate any attempt to store the power nor any suggestion of an alternative supply. When the wind stopped, everything stopped. Thus by habit if not by nature the Tazoons were probably nocturnal."

"But this is ridiculous," said Nevill. "I still can't conceive that they would fill whole plains with electrical generating transducers."

"Why not? They had no particular use for the great outdoors. By and large their native environment was intolerable to them."

Nevill sat up sharply. "That's a highly speculative statement to make. How do you arrive at that conclusion?"

"Simple," said Fritz. "Firstly, they were nearly blind, hence the need for such inordinately intense lighting such as we found on the subway. If my calculation is correct even Tazoo at mid-day was a pretty dull affair to their eyes. Secondly, the temperature the subway reached was so far above ambient that it's a reasonable guess that they couldn't tolerate outside temperatures for very long. They had a very low body mass and presumably chilled rapidly."

"Incredible!" said Nevill. "I knew they were small-boned, but body mass . . . ."

"If you'd seen the rates of acceleration and deceleration of a Tazoon subway train you'd soon see that only creatures of small body mass could survive it."

"All right," said Nash, "you seem to have all the answers. Perhaps you also know why the Tazoons became extinct?"

"I could make a good guess. Even more than ourselves the Tazoons were power dependent animals, for the aforementioned reasons. They had reached a point where they couldn't exist without power for light and heat, having presumably reached an evolutionary dead-end which had put them out of phase, so to speak, with their native environment. Now remember that they depended on power from the harps, not having any great resources of alternative fuels, either fossil or nuclear. Remember also that the harp frames were made of ironwood from the trees of the forest which used to adorn the plains. I suggest they increased their power generating areas at the expense of the trees until at some point they encountered soil erosion. Normally soil erosion is reversible if the right steps are taken to combat it, but..."

"Well?" said Nash.

"Soil erosion led to sand and the sand and wind conspired to form a sandblast which abraded and destroyed the strings of the harps. The failure of the harps meant loss of power—the very power essential to bring in the purified sea-water necessary to help combat the soil erosion. The process developed into a vicious circle—more sand, less harps; less harps, more sand, and so on *ad infinitum,* every day the situation worsening as the sand robbed them of the power they needed to combat its formation. When the sand grew deep enough it even prevented ironwood seeds from rooting, so the rest of the forests gradually died also. The Tazoons, faced with a gradual but unalterable loss of power, took the only course open to them—they tried to migrate to the tropical regions where the climate was life-supporting without the need for power. History seems to record that very few of them ever got there, which is not surprising when you consider that the night-wind was certainly capable of blowing a Tazoon clean into the air."

There was several moments' silence. "And the harps?" asked Nash. "That was their sole means of power generation?"

"We have found nothing which would indicate otherwise."

"What a pity! Philip Nevill had just succeeded in persuading me to lend support for a rather ambitious project. Consequent upon your demonstration of both power production and a potential source of transport, Philip was proposing to re-establish the Tazoon city, initially to cater for archaeologists interested in extra-terrestrial work, but later as a permanent colony and as a supply base for ships moving out to the Rim."

"You mean to repopulate the place—turn it back into a living city?"

"Given time, yes. If possible also irrigate the deserts and reclaim some of the wasteland. It's a great pity you have such admirable reasons why it can't be done."

"But it can be done," said Fritz. "Given time and sufficient labour to repair the harps there's enough energy out there to power the whole city and a dozen others."

"But I thought the sandblast . . ."

". . . . ruined the harp strings. Yes, it did . . . but that was before the advent of Fritz Van Noon. The Tazoons probably used a plain metal wire, possibly titanium, which was susceptible to abrasion. Remember they had no organic chemistry to speak of, hence no plastics. We're using a high tensile and extremely tough steel wire and a poly-silicone elastomer coating over it, which is a highly abrasion-resistant combination and should give many years' service without trouble. Unfortunately it damps the vibrations considerably—but then, we don't need the degree of either heat or light which the Tazoons found necessary."

"And you really believe the Tazoons became extinct because of the lack of a suitably coated wire?"

"Yes," said Fritz, "just that. And let it be a lesson to ourselves. We don't know what factors in our own technology may be lacking when it comes to meeting some new and unexpected crisis. Our development is probably as one-sided as the Tazoons, but in another direction. Therefore nothing but benefit can come from the complete assimilation of every phase of Tazoon science and technology into our own. If colonization can do that, then I'll see you have the power to colonize."

"For the want of a nail . . ." said Nevill speculatively.

"Fritz," said Nash. "I've been meaning to speak to you about the possibility of permanently establishing U.E. as a branch of the Terran Exploratory task force instead of merely a section of the Engineering Reserve. How would you react to that? Of course, it would mean promotion. . . ."

"I should personally welcome the idea, sir," said Fritz, "but I fear I've already accepted another assignment on Tiberius Two. They're trying to establish a mono-rail system there."

"I see," said Nash. "And just what is there about a mono-rail system on Tiberius Two that requires your peculiar talents?"

Fritz coughed discreetly. "I understand it's something to do with their gravity. Apparently it changes direction by seventy degrees every Tuesday and Thursday morning," he said, reaching for his cap.

The Machine Stops

E. M. FORSTER

This story paints a picture of an ultimate, mechanistic culture—horrifying in its existence and horrifying in its end. The story was written a long time ago (before the First World War), but many features of the world E. M. Forster describes are disconcertingly familiar today. Have the past sixty years brought us that much closer to The Machine?

PART 1: THE AIR-SHIP

Imagine, if you can, a small room, hexagonal in shape like the cell of a bee. It is lighted neither by window nor by lamp, yet it is filled with a soft radiance. There are no apertures for ventilation, yet the air is fresh. There are no musical instruments, and yet, at the moment that my meditation opens, this room is throbbing with melodious sounds. An arm-chair is in the centre, by its side a reading-desk—that is all the furniture. And in the arm-chair there sits a swaddled lump of flesh—a woman, about five feet high, with a face as white as a fungus. It is to her that the little room belongs.

An electric bell rang.

The woman touched a switch and the music was silent.

"I suppose I must see who it is," she thought, and set her chair in motion. The chair, like the music, was worked by machinery, and it rolled her to the other side of the room, where the bell still rang importunately.

"Who is it?" she called. Her voice was irritable, for she had been interrupted often since the music began. She knew several thousand people; in certain directions human intercourse had advanced enormously.

But when she listened into the receiver, her white face wrinkled into smiles, and she said:

"Very well. Let us talk, I will isolate myself. I do not

expect anything important will happen for the next five minutes—for I can give you fully five minutes, Kuno. Then I must deliver my lecture on 'Music during the Australian Period'."

She touched the isolation knob, so that no one else could speak to her. Then she touched the lighting apparatus, and the little room was plunged into darkness.

"Be quick!" she called, her irritation returning. "Be quick, Kuno; here I am in the dark wasting my time."

But it was fully fifteen seconds before the round plate that she held in her hands began to glow. A faint blue light shot across it, darkening to purple, and presently she could see the image of her son, who lived on the other side of the earth, and he could see her.

"Kuno, how slow you are."

He smiled gravely.

"I really believe you enjoy dawdling."

"I have called you before, mother, but you were always busy or isolated. I have something particular to say."

"What is it, dearest boy? Be quick. Why could you not send it by pneumatic post?"

"Because I prefer saying such a thing. I want—"

"Well?"

"I want you to come and see me."

Vashti watched his face in the blue plate.

"But I can see you!" she exclaimed. "What more do you want?"

"I want to see you not through the Machine," said Kuno. "I want to speak to you not through the wearisome Machine."

"Oh, hush!" said his mother, vaguely shocked. "You mustn't say anything against the Machine."

"Why not?"

"One mustn't."

"You talk as if a god had made the Machine," cried the other. "I believe that you pray to it when you are unhappy. Men made it, do not forget that. Great men, but men. The Machine is much, but it is not everything. I see something like you in this plate, but I do not see you. I hear something like you through this telephone, but I do not hear you.

That is why I want you to come. Come and stop with me. Pay me a visit, so that we can meet face to face, and talk about the hopes that are in my mind."

She replied that she could scarcely spare the time for a visit.

"The air-ship barely takes two days to fly between me and you."

"I dislike air-ships."

"Why?"

"I dislike seeing the horrible brown earth, and the sea, and the stars when it is dark. I get no ideas in an air-ship."

"I do not get them anywhere else."

"What kind of ideas can the air give you?"

He paused for an instant.

"Do you not know four big stars that form an oblong, and three stars close together in the middle of the oblong, and hanging from these stars, three other stars?"

"No, I do not. I dislike the stars. But did they give you an idea? How interesting; tell me."

"I had an idea that they were like a man."

"I do not understand."

"The four big stars are the man's shoulders and his knees. The three stars in the middle are like the belts that men wore once, and the three stars hanging are like a sword."

"A sword?"

"Men carried swords about with them, to kill animals and other men."

"It does not strike me as a very good idea, but it is certainly original. When did it come to you first?"

"In the air-ship—" He broke off, and she fancied that he looked sad. She could not be sure, for the Machine did not transmit *nuances* of expression. It only gave a general idea of people—an idea that was good enough for all practical purposes, Vashti thought. The imponderable bloom, declared by a discredited philosophy to be the actual essence of intercourse, was rightly ignored by the Machine, just as the imponderable bloom of the grape was ignored by the manufacturers of artificial fruit. Something "good enough" had long since been accepted by our race.

"The truth is," he continued, "that I want to see these

stars again. They are curious stars. I want to see them not from the air-ship, but from the surface of the earth, as our ancestors did, thousands of years ago. I want to visit the surface of the earth."

She was shocked again.

"Mother, you must come, if only to explain to me what is the harm of visiting the surface of the earth."

"No harm," she replied, controlling herself. "But no advantage. The surface of the earth is only dust and mud, no life remains on it, and you would need a respirator, or the cold of the outer air would kill you. One dies immediately in the outer air."

"I know; of course I shall take all precautions."

"And besides—"

"Well?"

She considered, and chose her words with care. Her son had a queer temper, and she wished to dissuade him from the expedition.

"It is contrary to the spirit of the age," she asserted.

"Do you mean by that, contrary to the Machine?"

"In a sense, but—"

His image in the blue plate faded.

"Kuno!"

He had isolated himself.

For a moment Vashti felt lonely.

Then she generated the light, and the sight of her room, flooded with radiance and studded with electric buttons, revived her. There were buttons and switches everywhere— buttons to call for food, for music, for clothing. There was the hot-bath button, by pressure of which a basin of (imitation) marble rose out of the floor, filled to the brim with a warm deodorized liquid. There was the cold-bath button. There was the button that produced literature. And there were of course the buttons by which she communicated with her friends. The room, though it contained nothing, was in touch with all she cared for in the world.

Vashti's next move was to turn off the isolation-switch, and all the accumulations of the last three minutes burst upon her. The room was filled with the noise of bells, and speaking-tubes. What was the new food like? Could she recommend it? Had she had any ideas lately? Might one tell her one's own ideas? Would she make an engagement to visit the public nurseries at an early date?—say this day month.

To most of these questions she replied with irritation—a growing quality in that accelerated age. She said that the new food was horrible. That she could not visit the public nurseries through press of engagements. That she had no idea of her own but had just been told one—that four stars and three in the middle were like a man: she doubted there was much in it. Then she switched off her correspondents, for it was time to deliver her lecture on Australian music.

The clumsy system of public gatherings had been long since abandoned; neither Vashti nor her audience stirred from their rooms. Seated in her arm-chair she spoke, while they in their arm-chairs heard her, fairly well, and saw her, fairly well. She opened with a humorous account of music in the pre-Mongolian epoch, and went on to describe the great outburst of song that followed the Chinese conquest. Remote and primeval as were the methods of I-San-So and the Brisbane school, she yet felt (she said) that study of them might repay the musician of today: they had freshness; they had, above all, ideas.

Her lecture, which lasted ten minutes, was well received and at its conclusion she and many of her audience listened to a lecture on the sea; there were ideas to be got from the sea; the speaker had donned a respirator and visited it lately. Then she fed, talked to many friends, had a bath, talked again, and summoned her bed.

The bed was not to her liking. It was too large, and she had a feeling for a small bed. Complaint was useless, for beds were of the same dimension all over the world, and to have had an alternative size would have involved vast alterations in the Machine. Vashti isolated herself—it was necessary, for neither day nor night existed under the ground—and reviewed all that had happened since she had summoned the bed last. Ideas? Scarcely any. Events—was Kuno's invitation an event?

By her side, on the little reading-desk, was a survival from the ages of litter—one book. This was the Book of the

Machine. In it were instructions against every possible contingency. If she was hot or cold or dyspeptic or at a loss for a word, she went to the book, and it told her which button to press. The Central Committee published it. In accordance with a growing habit, it was richly bound.

Sitting up in bed, she took it reverently in her hands. She glanced round the glowing room as if someone might be watching her. Then, ashamed, half joyful, she murmured "O Machine! O Machine!" and raised the volume to her lips. Thrice she kissed it, thrice inclined her head, thrice she felt the delirium of acquiescence. Her ritual performed, she turned to page 1367, which gave the times of the departure of the air-ships from the island in the southern hemisphere, under whose soil she lived, to the island in the northern hemisphere, whereunder lived her son.

She thought, "I have not the time."

She made the room dark and slept; she awoke and made the room light; she ate and exchanged ideas with her friends, and listened to music and attended lectures; she made the room dark and slept. Above her, beneath her, and around her, the Machine hummed eternally; she did not notice the noise, for she had been born with it in her ears. The earth, carrying her, hummed as it sped through silence, turning her now to the invisible sun, now to the invisible stars. She awoke and made the room light.

"Kuno!"

"I will not talk to you," he answered, "until you come."

"Have you been on the surface of the earth since we spoke last?"

His image faded.

Again she consulted the book. She became very nervous and lay back in her chair palpitating. Think of her as without teeth or hair. Presently she directed the chair to the wall, and pressed an unfamiliar button. The wall swung apart slowly. Through the opening she saw a tunnel that curved slightly, so that its goal was not visible. Should she go to see her son, here was the beginning of the journey.

Of course she knew all about the communication-system. There was nothing mysterious in it. She would summon a car and it would fly with her down the tunnel until it reached the lift that communicated with the air-ship station: the system had been in use for many, many years, long before the universal establishment of the Machine. And of course she had studied the civilization that had immediately preceded her own—the civilization that had mistaken the functions of the system, and had used it for bringing people to things, instead of for bringing things to people. Those funny old days, when men went for change of air instead of changing the air in their rooms! And yet—she was frightened of the tunnel: she had not seen it since her last child was born. It curved—but not quite as she remembered; it was brilliant—but not quite as brilliant as a lecturer had suggested. Vashti was seized with the terrors of direct experience. She shrank back into the room, and the wall closed up again.

"Kuno," she said, "I cannot come to see you. I am not well."

Immediately an enormous apparatus fell on to her out of the ceiling, a thermometer was automatically inserted between her lips, a stethoscope was automatically laid upon her heart. She lay powerless. Cool pads soothed her forehead. Kuno had telegraphed to her doctor.

So the human passions still blundered up and down in the Machine. Vashti drank the medicine that the doctor projected into her mouth, and the machinery retired into the ceiling. The voice of Kuno was heard asking how she felt.

"Better." Then with irritation: "But why do you not come to me instead?"

"Because I cannot leave this place."

"Why?"

"Because, any moment, something tremendous may happen."

"Have you been on the surface of the earth yet?"

"Not yet."

"Then what is it?"

"I will not tell you through the machine."

She resumed her life.

But she thought of Kuno as a baby, his birth, his removal to the public nurseries, her one visit to him there, his visits to her—visits which stopped when the Machine had assigned him a room on the other side of the earth. "Parents, duties of," said the book of the Machine, "cease at the moment of birth. P. 422327483." True, but there was something special about Kuno—indeed there had been something special about all her children—and, after all, she must brave the journey if he desired it. And "something tremendous might happen". What did that mean? The nonsense of a youthful man, no doubt, but she must go. Again she pressed the unfamiliar button, again the wall swung back, and she saw the tunnel that curved out of sight. Clasping the Book, she rose, tottered on to the platform, and summoned the car. Her room closed behind her: the journey to the northern hemisphere had begun.

Of course it was perfectly easy. The car approached and in it she found arm-chairs exactly like her own. When she signalled, it stopped, and she tottered into the lift. One other passenger was in the lift, the first fellow creature she had seen face to face for months. Few travelled in these days, for, thanks to the advance of science, the earth was exactly alike all over. Rapid intercourse, from which the previous civilization had hoped so much, had ended by defeating itself. What was the good of going to Pekin when it was just like Shrewsbury? Why return to Shrewsbury when it would be just like Pekin? Men seldom moved their bodies; all unrest was concentrated in the soul.

The air-ship service was a relic from the former age. It was kept up, because it was easier to keep it up than to stop it or to diminish it, but it now far exceeded the wants of the population. Vessel after vessel would rise from the vomitories of Rye or of Christchurch (I use the antique names), would sail into the crowded sky, and would draw up at the wharves of the south—empty. So nicely adjusted was the system, so independent of meteorology, that the sky, whether calm or cloudy, resembled a vast kaleidoscope whereon the same patterns periodically recurred. The ship on which Vashti sailed started now at sunset, now at dawn. But always, as it passed above Rheims, it would neighbour the ship that served between Helsingfors and the Brazils, and, every third time it surmounted the Alps, the fleet of Palermo would cross its track behind. Night and day, wind and storm, tide and earthquake, impeded man no longer. He had harnessed Leviathan. All the old literature, with its praise of Nature and its fear of Nature, rang false as the prattle of a child.

Yet as Vashti saw the vast flank of the ship, stained with exposure to the outer air, her horror of direct experience returned. It was not quite like the air-ship in the cinematophote. For one thing it smelt—not strongly or unpleasantly, but it did smell, and with her eyes shut she should have known that a new thing was close to her. Then she had to walk to it from the lift, had to submit to glances from the other passengers. The man in front dropped his Book—no great matter, but it disquieted them all. In the rooms, if the Book was dropped, the floor raised it mechanically, but the gangway to the air-ship was not so prepared, and the sacred volume lay motionless. They stopped—the thing was unforeseen—and the man, instead of picking up his property, felt the muscles of his arm to see how they had failed him. Then someone actually said with direct utterance: "We shall be late"—and they trooped on board, Vashti treading on the pages as she did so.

Inside, her anxiety increased. The arrangements were old-fashioned and rough. There was even a female attendant, to whom she would have to announce her wants during the voyage. Of course a revolving platform ran the length of the boat, but she was expected to walk from it to her cabin. Some cabins were better than others, and she did not get the best. She thought the attendant had been unfair, and spasms of rage shook her. The glass valves had closed, she could not go back. She saw, at the end of the vestibule, the lift in which she had ascended going quietly up and down, empty. Beneath those corridors of shining tiles were rooms, tier below tier, reaching far into the earth, and in each room there sat a human being, eating, or sleeping, or producing ideas. And buried deep in the hive was her own room. Vashti was afraid.

"O Machine! O Machine!" she murmured, and caressed her Book, and was comforted.

Then the sides of the vestibule seemed to melt together,

as do the passages that we see in dreams, the lift vanished, the Book that had been dropped slid to the left and vanished, polished tiles rushed by like a stream of water, there was a slight jar, and the air-ship, issuing from its tunnel, soared above the waters of a tropical ocean.

It was night. For a moment she saw the coast of Sumatra edged by the phosphorescence of waves, and crowned by lighthouses, still sending forth their disregarded beams. These also vanished, and only the stars distracted her. They were not motionless, but swayed to and fro above her head, thronging out of one skylight into another, as if the universe and not the air-ship was careening. And, as often happens on clear nights, they seemed now to be in perspective, now on a plane; now piled tier beyond tier into the infinite heavens, now concealing infinity, a roof limiting for ever the visions of men. In either case they seemed intolerable. "Are we to travel in the dark?" called the passengers angrily, and the attendant, who had been careless, generated the light and pulled down the blinds of pliable metal. When the air-ships had been built, the desire to look direct at things still lingered in the world. Hence the extraordinary number of skylights and windows, and the proportionate discomfort to those who were civilized and refined. Even in Vashti's cabin one star peeped through a flaw in the blind, and after a few hours' uneasy slumber, she was disturbed by an unfamiliar glow, which was the dawn.

Quick as the ship had sped westwards, the earth had rolled eastwards quicker still, and had dragged back Vashti and her companions towards the sun. Science could prolong the night, but only for a little, and those high hopes of neutralizing the earth's diurnal revolution had passed, together with hopes that were possibly higher. To "keep pace with the sun", or even to outstrip it, had been the aim of the civilization preceding this. Racing aeroplanes had been built for the purpose, capable of enormous speed, and steered by the greatest intellects of the epoch. Round the globe they went, round and round, westward, westward, round and round, amidst humanity's applause. In vain. The globe went eastward quicker still, horrible accidents occurred, and the Committee of the Machine, at the time rising into prominence, declared the pursuit illegal, unmechanical, and punishable by Homelessness.

Of Homelessness more will be said later.

Doubtless the Committee was right. Yet the attempt to "defeat the sun" aroused the last common interest that our race experienced about the heavenly bodies, or indeed about anything. It was the last time that men were compacted by thinking of a power outside the world. The sun had conquered, yet it was the end of his spiritual dominion. Dawn, midday, twilight, the zodiacal path, touched neither men's lives nor their hearts, and science retreated into the ground, to concentrate herself upon problems that she was certain of solving.

So when Vashti found her cabin invaded by a rosy finger of light, she was annoyed and tried to adjust the blind. But the blind flew up altogether, and she saw through the skylight small pink clouds, swaying against a background of blue, and as the sun crept higher, its radiance entered direct, brimming down the wall, like a golden sea. It rose and fell with the air-ship's motion, just as waves rise and fall, but it advanced steadily, as a tide advances. Unless she was careful, it would strike her face. A spasm of horror shook her and she rang for the attendant. The attendant too was horrified, but she could do nothing; it was not her place to mend the blind. She could only suggest that the lady should change her cabin, which she accordingly prepared to do.

People were almost exactly alike all over the world, but the attendant of the air-ship, perhaps owing to her exceptional duties, had grown a little out of the common. She had often to address passengers with direct speech, and this had given her a certain roughness and originality of manner. When Vashti swerved away from the sunbeams with a cry, she behaved barbarically—she put out her hand to steady her.

"How dare you!" exclaimed the passenger. "You forget yourself!"

The woman was confused, and apologized for not having let her fall. People never touched one another. The custom had become obsolete, owing to the Machine.

"Where are we now?" asked Vashti haughtily.

"We are over Asia," said the attendant, anxious to be polite.

"Asia?"

"You must excuse my common way of speaking. I have got into the habit of calling places over which I pass by their unmechanical names."

"Oh, I remember Asia. The Mongols came from it."

"Beneath us, in the open air, stood a city that was once called Simla."

"Have you ever heard of the Mongols and of the Brisbane school?"

"No."

"Brisbane also stood in the open air."

"Those mountains to the right—let me show you them." She pushed back a metal blind. The main chain of the Himalayas was revealed. "They were once called the Roof of the World, those mountains."

"What a foolish name!"

"You must remember that, before the dawn of civilization, they seemed to be an impenetrable wall that touched the stars. It was supposed that no one but the gods could exist above their summits. How we have advanced, thanks to the Machine!"

"How we have advanced, thanks to the Machine!" said Vashti.

"How we have advanced, thanks to the Machine!" echoed the passenger who had dropped his Book the night before and who was standing in the passage.

"And that white stuff in the cracks?—what is it?"

"I have forgotten its name."

"Cover the window, please. These mountains give me no ideas."

The northern aspect of the Himalayas was in deep shadow: on the Indian slope the sun had just prevailed. The forests had been destroyed during the literature epoch for the purpose of making newspaper-pulp, but the snows were awakening to their morning glory, and clouds still hung on the breasts of Kangchenjunga. In the plain were seen the ruins of cities, with diminished rivers creeping by their walls, and by the sides of these were sometimes the signs of vomitories, marking the cities of today. Over the whole prospect air-ships rushed, crossing and inter-crossing with incredible *aplomb,* and rising nonchalantly when they desired to escape the perturbations of the lower atmosphere and to traverse the Roof of the World.

"We have indeed advanced, thanks to the Machine," repeated the attendant, and hid the Himalayas behind a metal blind.

The day dragged wearily forward. The passengers sat each in his cabin, avoiding one another with an almost physical repulsion and longing to be once more under the surface of the earth. There were eight or ten of them, mostly young males, sent out from the public nurseries to inhabit the rooms of those who had died in various parts of the earth. The man who had dropped his Book was on the homeward journey. He had been sent to Sumatra for the purpose of propagating the race. Vashti alone was travelling by her private will.

At midday she took a second glance at the earth. The air-ship was crossing another range of mountains, but she could see little, owing to clouds. Masses of black rock hovered below her and merged indistinctly into grey. Their shapes were fantastic; one of them resembled a prostrate man.

"No ideas here," murmured Vashti, and hid the Caucasus behind a metal blind.

In the evening she looked again. They were crossing a golden sea, in which lay many small islands and one peninsula.

She repeated, "No ideas here," and hid Greece behind a metal blind.

PART II: THE MENDING APPARATUS

By a vestibule, by a lift, by a tubular railway, by a platform, by a sliding door—by reversing all the steps of her departure did Vashti arrive at her son's room, which exactly resembled her own. She might well declare that the visit was superfluous. The buttons, the knobs, the reading-desk with the Book, the temperature, the atmosphere, the illumination—all were exactly the same. And if Kuno himself, flesh of her flesh, stood close beside her at last, what profit was there in that? She was too well-bred to shake him by the hand.

Averting her eyes, she spoke as follows:

"Here I am. I have had the most terrible journey and greatly retarded the development of my soul. It is not worth it, Kuno, it is not worth it. My time is too precious. The sunlight almost touched me, and I have met with the rudest people. I can only stop a few minutes. Say what you want to say, and then I must return."

"I have been threatened with Homelessness," said Kuno.

She looked at him now.

"I have been threatened with Homelessness, and I could not tell you such a thing through the Machine."

Homelessness means death. The victim is exposed to the air, which kills him.

"I have been outside since I spoke to you last. The tremendous thing has happened, and they have discovered me."

"But why shouldn't you go outside?" she exclaimed. "It is perfectly legal, perfectly mechanical, to visit the surface of the earth. I have lately been to a lecture on the sea; there is no objection to that; one simply summons a respirator and gets an Egression-permit. It is not the kind of thing that spiritually-minded people do, and I begged you not to do it, but there is no legal objection to it."

"I did not get an Egression-permit."

"Then how did you get out?"

"I found out a way of my own."

The phrase conveyed no meaning to her, and he had to repeat it.

"A way of your own?" she whispered. "But that would be wrong."

"Why?"

The question shocked her beyond measure.

"You are beginning to worship the Machine," he said

coldly. "You think it irreligious of me to have found out a way of my own. It was just what the Committee thought, when they threatened me with Homelessness."

At this she grew angry. "I worship nothing!" she cried. "I am most advanced. I don't think you irreligious, for there is no such thing as religion left. All the fear and the superstition that existed once have been destroyed by the Machine. I only meant that to find out a way of your own was—Besides, there is no new way out."

"So it is always supposed."

"Except through the vomitories, for which one must have an Egression-permit, it is impossible to get out. The Book says so."

"Well, the Book's wrong, for I have been out on my feet."

For Kuno was possessed of a certain physical strength.

By these days it was a demerit to be muscular. Each infant was examined at birth, and all who promised undue strength were destroyed. Humanitarians may protest, but it would have been no true kindness to let an athlete live; he would never have been happy in that state of life to which the Machine had called him; he would have yearned for trees to climb, rivers to bathe in, meadows and hills against which he might measure his body. Man must be adapted to his surroundings, must he not? In the dawn of the world our weaklings must be exposed on Mount Taygetus, in its twilight our strong will suffer euthanasia, that the Machine may progress eternally.

"You know that we have lost the sense of space. We say 'space is annihilated', but we have annihilated not space but the sense thereof. We have lost a part of ourselves. I determined to recover it, and I began by walking up and down the platform of the railway outside my room. Up and down, until I was tired, and so did recapture the meaning of 'Near' and 'Far'. 'Near' is a place to which I can get quickly *on my feet,* not a place to which the train or the airship will take me quickly. 'Far' is a place to which I cannot get quickly on my feet; the vomitory is 'far', though I could be there in thirty-eight seconds by summoning the train. Man is the measure. That was my first lesson. Man's feet are the measure for distance, his hands are the measure for ownership, his body is the measure for all that is lovable and desirable and strong. Then I went further: it was then that I called to you for the first time, and you would not come."

"This city, as you know, is built deep beneath the surface of the earth, with only the vomitories protruding. Having paced the platform outside my own room, I took the lift to the next platform and paced that also, and so with each in turn, until I came to the topmost, above which begins the earth. All the platforms were exactly alike, and all that I gained by visiting them was to develop my sense of space and my muscles. I think I should have been content with this—it is not a little thing—but as I walked and brooded, it occurred to me that our cities had been built in the days when men still breathed the outer air, and that there had been ventilation shafts for the workmen. I could think of nothing but these ventilation shafts. Had they been destroyed by all the food-tubes and medicine-tubes and music-tubes that the Machine has evolved lately? Or did traces of them remain? One thing was certain. If I came upon them anywhere, it would be in the railway-tunnels of the topmost storey. Everywhere else, all space was accounted for.

"I am telling my story quickly, but don't think that I was not a coward or that your answers never depressed me. It is not the proper thing, it is not mechanical, it is not decent to walk along a railway-tunnel. I did not fear that I might tread upon a live rail and be killed. I feared something far more intangible—doing what was not contemplated by the Machine. Then I said to myself, 'Man is the measure', and I went, and after many visits I found an opening.

"The tunnels, of course, were lighted. Everything is light, artificial light; darkness is the exception. So when I saw a black gap in the tiles, I knew that it was an exception, and rejoiced. I put in my arm—I could put in no more at first—and waved it round and round in ecstasy. I loosened another tile, and put in my head, and shouted into the darkness: 'I am coming, I shall do it yet', and my voice reverberated down endless passages. I seemed to hear the spirits of those dead workmen who had returned each evening to the starlight and to their wives, and all the generations who had lived in the open air called back to me, 'You will do it yet, you are coming'."

He paused, and, absurd as he was, his last words moved her. For Kuno had lately asked to be a father, and his request had been refused by the Committee. His was not a type that the Machine desired to hand on.

"Then a train passed. It brushed by me, but I thrust my head and arms into the hole. I had done enough for one day, so I crawled back to the platform, went down in the lift, and summoned my bed. Ah, what dreams! And again I called you, and again you refused."

She shook her head and said:

"Don't. Don't talk of these terrible things. You make me miserable. You are throwing civilization away."

"But I had got back the sense of space and a man cannot rest then. I determined to get in at the hole and climb the shaft. And so I exercised my arms. Day after day I went through ridiculous movements, until my flesh ached, and I could hang by my hands and hold the pillow of my bed outstretched for many minutes. then I summoned a respirator, and started.

"It was easy at first. The mortar had somehow rotted, and I soon pushed some more tiles in, and clambered after them into the darkness, and the spirits of the dead comforted me. I don't know what I mean by that. I just say what I felt. I felt, for the first time, that a protest had been lodged against corruption, and that even as the dead were comforting me, so I was comforting the unborn. I felt that humanity existed, and that it existed without clothes. How can I possibly explain this? It was naked, humanity seemed naked, and all these tubes and buttons and machineries neither came into the world with us, nor will they follow us out, nor do they matter supremely while we are here. Had I been strong, I would have torn off every garment I had, and gone out into the outer air unswaddled. But this is not for me, nor perhaps for my generation. I climbed with my respirator and my hygienic clothes and my dietetic tabloids! Better thus than not at all.

"There was a ladder, made of some primeval metal. The light from the railway fell upon its lowest rungs, and I saw that it led straight upwards out of the rubble at the bottom of the shaft. Perhaps our ancestors ran up and down it a dozen times daily, in their building. As I climbed, the rough edges cut through my gloves so that my hands bled. The light helped me for a little, and then came darkness and, worse still, silence which pierced my ears like a sword. The Machine hums! Did you know that? Its hum penetrates our blood, and may even guide our thoughts. Who knows! I was getting beyond its power. Then I thought: 'This silence means that I am doing wrong.' But I heard voices in the silence, and again they strengthened me.' He laughed. "I had need of them. The next moment I cracked my head against something."

She sighed.

"I had reached one of those pneumatic stoppers that defend us from the outer air. You may have noticed them on the air-ship. Pitch dark, my feet on the rungs of an invisible ladder, my hands out, I cannot explain how I lived through this part, but the voices still comforted me, and I felt for fastenings. The stopper, I suppose, was about eight feet across. I passed my hand over it as far as I could reach. It was perfectly smooth. I felt it almost to the centre. Not quite to the centre, for my arm was too short. Then the voice said: 'Jump. It is worth it. There may be a handle in the centre, and you may catch hold of it and so come to us your own way. And if there is no handle, so that you may fall and are dashed to pieces—it is still worth it: you will still come to us your own way.' So I jumped. There was a handle, and—"

He paused. Tears gathered in his mother's eyes. She knew that he was fated. If he did not die today he would die tomorrow. There was not room for such a person in the world. And with her pity disgust mingled. She was ashamed at having borne such a son, she who had always been so respectable and so full of ideas. Was he really the little boy to whom she had taught the use of his stops and buttons, and to whom she had given his first lessons in the Book? The very hair that disfigured his lip showed that he was reverting to some savage type. On atavism the Machine can have no mercy.

"There was a handle, and I did catch it. I hung tranced over the darkness and heard the hum of these workings as the last whisper in a dying dream. All the things I had cared about and all the people I had spoken to through tubes appeared infinitely little. Meanwhile the handle revolved. My weight had set something in motion and I span slowly, and then—

"I cannot describe it. I was lying with my face to the sunshine. Blood poured from my nose and ears and I heard a tremendous roaring. The stopper, with me clinging to it, had simply been blown out of the earth, and the air that we make down here was escaping through the vent into the air above. It burst up like a fountain. I crawled back to it—for the upper air hurts—and, as it were, I took great sips from the edge. My respirator had flown goodness knows where, my clothes were torn. I just lay with my lips close to the hole, and I sipped until the bleeding stopped. You can imagine nothing so curious. This hollow in the grass—I will speak of it in a minute—the sun shining into it, not brilliantly but through marbled clouds—the peace, the nonchalance, the sense of space, and, brushing my cheek, the roaring fountain of our artificial air! Soon I spied my respirator, bobbing up and down in the current high above my head, and higher still were many air-ships. But no one ever looks out of air-ships, and in any case they could not have picked me up. There I was, stranded. The sun shone a little way down the shaft, and revealed the topmost rung of the ladder, but it was hopeless trying to reach it. I should either have been tossed up again by the escape, or else have fallen in, and died. I could only lie on the grass, sipping and sipping, and from time to time glancing around me.

"I knew that I was in Wessex, for I had taken care to go to a lecture on the subject before starting. Wessex lies above the room in which we are talking now. It was once an important state. Its kings held all the southern coast from the Andredswald to Cornwall, while the Wansdyke protected them on the north, running over the high ground. The lecturer was only concerned with the rise of Wessex, so I do not know how long it remained an international power, nor would the knowledge have assisted me. To tell the truth, I could do nothing but laugh during this part. There was I, with a pneumatic stopper by my side and a respirator bobbing over my head, imprisoned, all three of us, in a grass-grown hollow that was edged with fern."

Then he grew grave again.

"Lucky for me that it was a hollow. For the air began to fall back into it and to fill it as water fills a bowl. I could crawl about. Presently I stood. I breathed a mixture, in which the air that hurts predominated whenever I tried to climb the sides. This was not so bad. I had not lost my tabloids and remained ridiculously cheerful, and as for the Machine, I forgot about it altogether. My one aim now was to get to the top, where the ferns were, and to view whatever objects lay beyond.

"I rushed the slope. The new air was still too bitter for me and I came rolling back, after a momentary vision of something grey. The sun grew very feeble, and I remembered that he was in Scorpio—I had been to a lecture on that too. If the sun is in Scorpio and you are in Wessex, it means that you must be as quick as you can or it will get too dark. (This is the first bit of useful information I have ever got from a lecture, and I expect it will be the last.) It made me try frantically to breathe the new air, and to advance as far as I dared out of my pond. The hollow filled so slowly. At times I thought that the fountain played with less vigour. My respirator seemed to dance nearer the earth; the roar was decreasing."

He broke off.

"I don't think this is interesting you. The rest will interest you even less. There are no ideas in it, and I wish that I had not troubled you to come. We are too different, mother."

She told him to continue.

"It was evening before I climbed the bank. The sun had very nearly slipped out of the sky by this time, and I could not get a good view. You, who have just crossed the Roof of the World, will not want to hear an account of the little hills that I saw—low colourless hills. But to me they were living and the turf that covered them was a skin, under which their muscles rippled, and I felt that those hills had called with incalculable force to men in the past, and that men had loved them. Now they sleep—perhaps for ever. They commune with humanity in dreams. Happy the man, happy the woman, who awakes the hills of Wessex. For though they sleep, they will never die."

His voice rose passionately.

"Cannot you see, cannot all you lecturers see, that it is we that are dying, and that down here the only thing that really lives is the Machine? We created the Machine, to do our will, but we cannot make it do our will now. It has robbed us of the sense of space and of the sense of touch, it has blurred every human relation and narrowed down love to a carnal act, it has paralysed our bodies and our wills, and now it compels us to worship it. The Machine develops—but not on our lines. The Machine proceeds—but not to our goal. We only exist as the blood corpuscles that course through its arteries, and if it could work without us, it would let us die. Oh, I have no remedy—or, at least, only one—to tell men again and again that I have seen the hills of Wessex as Aelfrid saw them when he overthrew the Danes.

"So the sun set. I forgot to mention that a belt of mist lay between my hill and other hills, and that it was the colour of pearl."

He broke off for the second time.

"Go on," said his mother wearily.

He shook his head.

"Go on. Nothing that you say can distress me now. I am hardened."

"I had meant to tell you the rest, but I cannot: I know that I cannot: good-bye."

Vashti stood irresolute. All her nerves were tingling with his blasphemies. But she was also inquisitive.

"This is unfair," she complained. "You have called me across the world to hear your story, and hear it I will. Tell me—as briefly as possible, for this is a disastrous waste of time—tell me how you returned to civilization."

"Oh—that!" he said, starting. "You would like to hear

about civilization. Certainly. Had I got to where my respirator fell down?"

"No—but I understand everything now. You put on your respirator, and managed to walk along the surface of the earth to a vomitory, and there your conduct was reported to the Central Committee."

"By no means."

He passed his hand over his forehead, as if dispelling some strong impression. Then, resuming his narrative, he warmed to it again.

"My respirator fell about sunset. I had mentioned that the fountain seemed feebler, had I not?"

"Yes."

"About sunset, it let the respirator fall. As I said, I had entirely forgotten about the Machine, and I paid no great attention at the time, being occupied with other things. I had my pool of air, into which I could dip when the outer keenness became intolerable, and which would possibly remain for days, provided that no wind sprang up to disperse it. Not until it was too late did I realize what the stoppage of the escape implied. You see--the gap in the tunnel had been mended; the Mending Apparatus; the Mending Apparatus, was after me.

"One other warning I had, but I neglected it. The sky at night was clearer than it had been in the day, and the moon, which was about half the sky behind the sun, shone into the dell at moments quite brightly. I was in my usual place—on the boundary between the two atmospheres—when I thought I saw something dark move across the bottom of the dell, and vanish into the shaft. In my folly, I ran down. I bent over and listened, and I thought I heard a faint scraping noise in the depths.

"At this—but it was too late—I took alarm. I determined to put on my respirator and to walk right out of the dell. But my respirator had gone. I knew exactly where it had fallen—between the stopper and the aperture—and I could even feel the mark that it had made in the turf. It had gone, and I realized that something evil was at work, and I had better escape to the other air, and, if I must die, die running towards the cloud that had been the colour of a pearl. I never started. Out of the shaft—it is too horrible. A worm, a long white worm, had crawled out of the shaft and was gliding over the moonlit grass.

"I screamed. I did everything that I should not have done, I stamped upon the creature instead of flying from it, and it at once curled round my ankle. Then we fought. The worm let me run all over the dell, but edged up my leg as I ran. 'Help!' I cried. (That part is too awful. It belongs to the part that you will never know.) 'Help!' I cried. (Why cannot we suffer in silence?) 'Help' I cried. Then my feet were wound together, I fell, I was dragged away from the dear ferns and the living hills, and past the great metal stopper (I can tell you this part), and I thought it might save me again if I caught hold of the handle. It also was enwrapped, it also. Oh, the whole dell was full of the things. They were searching it in all directions, they were denuding it, and the white snouts of others peeped out of the hole, ready if needed. Everything that could be moved they brought—brushwood, bundles of fern, everything, and down we all went intertwined into hell. The last things that I saw, ere the stopper closed after us, were certain stars, and I felt that a man of my sort lived in the sky. For I did fight, I fought till the very end, and it was only my head hitting against the ladder that quieted me. I woke up in this room. The worms had vanished, I was surrounded by artificial air, artificial light, artificial peace, and my friends were calling to me down speaking-tubes to know whether I had come across any new ideas lately."

Here his story ended. Discussion of it was impossible, and Vashti turned to go.

"It will end in Homelessness," she said quietly.

"I wish it would," retorted Kuno.

"The Machine has been most merciful."

"I prefer the mercy of God."

"By that superstitious phrase, do you mean that you could live in the outer air?"

"Yes."

"Have you ever seen, round the vomitories, the bones of those who were extruded after the Great Rebellion?"

"Yes."

"They were left where they perished for our edification. A few crawled away, but they perished, too—who can doubt it? And so with the Homeless of our own day. The surface of the earth supports life no longer."

"Indeed."

"Ferns and a little grass may survive, but all higher forms have perished. Has any air-ship detected them?"

"No."

"Has any lecturer dealt with them?"

"No."

"Then why this obstinacy?"

"Because I have seen them," he exploded.

"Seen *what*?"

"Because I have seen her in the twilight—because she came to my help when I called—because she, too, was entangled by the worms, and, luckier than I, was killed by one of them piercing her throat."

He was mad. Vashti departed, nor, in the troubles that followed, did she ever see his face again.

PART III: THE HOMELESS

During the years that followed Kuno's escapade, two important developments took place in the Machine. On the surface they were revolutionary, but in either case men's minds had been prepared beforehand, and they did but express tendencies that were latent already.

The first of these was the abolition of respirators.

Advanced thinkers, like Vashti, had always held it foolish to visit the surface of the earth. Air-ships might be necessary, but what was the good of going out for mere curiosity and crawling along for a mile or two in a terrestrial motor? The habit was vulgar and perhaps faintly improper: it was unproductive of ideas, and had no connexion with the habits that really mattered. So respirators were abolished, and with them, of course, the terrestrial motors, and except for a few lecturers, who complained that they were debarred access to their subject-matter, the development was accepted quietly. Those who still wanted to know what the earth was like had after all only to listen to some gramophone or to look into some cinematophote. And even the lecturers acquiesced when they found that a lecture on the sea was none the less stimulating when compiled out of other lectures that had already been delivered on the same subject. "Beware of first-hand ideas!" exclaimed one of the most advanced of them. "First-hand ideas do not really exist. They are but the physical impressions produced by love and fear, and on this gross foundation who could erect a philosophy? Let your ideas be second-hand, and if possible tenth-hand, for then they will be far removed from that disturbing element—direct observation. Do not learn anything about this subject of mine—the French Revolution. Learn instead what I think that Enicharmon thought Urizen thought Gutch thought Ho-Yung thought Chi-Bo-Sing thought Lafcadio Hearn thought Carlyle thought Mirabeau said about the French Revolution. Through the medium of these ten great minds the blood that was shed at Paris and the windows that were broken at Versailles will be clarified to an idea which you may employ most profitably in your daily lives. But be sure that the intermediates are many and varied, for in history one authority exists to counteract another. Urizen must counteract the scepticism of Ho-Yung and Enicharmon, I must myself counteract the impetuosity of Gutch. You who listen to me are in a better position to judge about the French Revolution than I am. Your descendants will be even in a better position than you, for they will learn what you think I think, and yet another intermediate will be added to the chain. And in time"—his voice rose—"there will come a generation that has got beyond facts, beyond impressions, a generation absolutely colourless, a generation

seraphically free
From taint of personality,

which will see the French Revolution not as it happened, nor as they would like it to have happened, but as it would have happened had it taken place in the days of the Machine."

Tremendous applause greeted this lecture, which did but

voice a feeling already latent in the minds of men—a feeling that terrestrial facts must be ignored, and that the abolition of respirators was a positive gain. It was even suggested that air-ships should be abolished too. This was not done, because air-ships had somehow worked themselves into the Machine's system. But year by year they were used less, and mentioned less by thoughtful men.

The second great development was the re-establishment of religion.

This, too, had been voiced in the celebrated lecture. No one could mistake the reverent tone in which the peroration had concluded, and it awakened a responsive echo in the heart of each. Those who had long worshipped silently now began to talk. They described the strange feeling of peace that came over them when they handled the Book of the Machine, the pleasure that it was to repeat certain numerals out of it, however little meaning those numerals conveyed to the outward ear, the ecstasy of touching a button however unimportant, or of ringing an electric bell however superfluously.

"The Machine," they exclaimed, "feeds us and clothes us and houses us; through it we speak to one another, through it we see one another, in it we have our being. The Machine is the friend of ideas and the enemy of superstition: the Machine is omnipotent, eternal; blessed is the Machine." And before long this allocution was printed on the first page of the Book, and in subsequent editions the ritual swelled into a complicated system of praise and prayer. The word "religion" was sedulously avoided, and in theory the Machine was still the creation and the implement of man. But in practice all, save a few retrogrades, worshipped it as divine. Nor was it worshipped in unity. One believer would be chiefly impressed by the blue optic plates, through which he saw other believers; another by the mending apparatus, which sinful Kuno had compared to worms; another by the lifts, another by the Book. And each would pray to this or to that, and ask it to intercede for him with the Machine as a whole. Persecution—that also was present. It did not break out, for reasons that will be set forward shortly. But it was

latent, and all who did not accept the minimum known as
"undenominational Mechanism" lived in danger of
Homelessness, which means death, as we know.

To attribute these two great developments to the Central
Committee is to take a very narrow view of civilization.
The Central Committee announced the developments, it is
true, but they were no more the cause of them than were
the kings of the imperialistic period the cause of war.
Rather did they yield to some invincible pressure, which
came no one knew whither, and which, when gratified, was
succeeded by some new pressure equally invincible. To
such a state of affairs it is convenient to give the name of
progress. No one confessed the Machine was out of hand.
Year by year it was served with increased efficiency and
decreased intelligence. The better a man knew his own
duties upon it, the less he understood the duties of his
neighbour, and in all the world there was not one who
understood the monster as a whole. Those master brains
had perished. They had left full directions, it is true, and
their successors had each of them mastered a portion of
those directions. But Humanity, in its desire for comfort,
had overreached itself. It had exploited the riches of nature
too far. Quietly and complacently, it was sinking into
decadence, and progress had come to mean the progress of
the Machine.

As for Vashti, her life went peacefully forward until the
final disaster. She made her room dark and slept; she
awoke and made the room light. She lectured and attended
lectures. She exchanged ideas with her innumerable friends
and believed she was growing more spiritual. At times a
friend was granted Euthanasia, and left his or her room for
the homelessness that is beyond all human conception.
Vashti did not much mind. After an unsuccessful lecture,
she would sometimes ask for Euthanasia herself. But the
death-rate was not permitted to exceed the birth-rate, and
the Machine had hitherto refused it to her.

The troubles began quietly, long before she was
conscious of them.

One day she was astonished at receiving a message from
her son. They never communicated, having nothing in

common, and she had only heard indirectly that he was still
alive, and had been transferred from the northern
hemisphere, where he had behaved so mischievously, to the
southern—indeed, to a room not far from her own.

"Does he want me to visit him?" she thought. "Never
again, never. And I have not the time."

No, it was madness of another kind.

He refused to visualize his face upon the blue plate, and
speaking out of the darkness with solemnity said:

"The Machine stops."

"What do you say?"

"The Machine is stopping, I know it, I know the signs."

She burst into a peal of laughter. He heard her and was
angry, and they spoke no more.

"Can you imagine anything more absurd?" she cried to
a friend. "A man who was my son believes that the
Machine is stopping. It would be impious if it was not
mad."

"The Machine is stopping?" her friend replied. "What
does that mean? The phrase conveys nothing to me."

"Nor to me."

"He does not refer, I suppose, to the trouble there has
been lately with the music?"

"Oh no, of course not. Let us talk about music."

"Have you complained to the authorities?"

"Yes, and they say it wants mending, and referred me to
the Committee of the Mending Apparatus. I complained of
those curious gasping sighs that disfigure the symphonies
of the Brisbane school. They sound like someone in pain.
The Committee of the Mending Apparatus say that it shall
be remedied shortly."

Obscurely worried, she resumed her life. For one thing,
the defect in the music irritated her. For another thing, she
could not forget Kuno's speech. If he had known that the
music was out of repair—he could not know it, for he
detested music—if he had known that it was wrong, "the
Machine stops" was exactly the venomous sort of remark he
would have made. Of course he had made it at a venture,
but the coincidence annoyed her, and she spoke with some
petulance to the Committee of the Mending Apparatus.

They replied, as before, that the defect would be set right shortly.

"Shortly! At once!" she retorted. "Why should I be worried by imperfect music? Things are always put right at once. If you do not mend it at once, I shall complain to the Central Committee."

"No personal complaints are received by the Central Committee," the Committee of the Mending Apparatus replied.

"Through whom am I to make my complaint, then?"

"Through us."

"I complain then."

"Your complaint shall be forwarded in its turn."

"Have others complained?"

This question was unmechanical, and the Committee of the Mending Apparatus refused to answer it.

"It is too bad!" she exclaimed to another of her friends. "There never was such an unfortunate woman as myself. I can never be sure of my music now. It gets worse and worse each time I summon it."

"I too have my troubles," the friend replied. "Sometimes my ideas are interrupted by a slight jarring noise."

"What is it?"

"I do not know whether it is inside my head or inside the wall."

"Complain in either case."

"I have complained, and my complaint will be forwarded in its turn to the Central Committee."

Time passed, and they resented the defects no longer. The defects had not been remedied, but the human tissues in that latter day had become so subservient that they readily adapted themselves to every caprice of the Machine. The sigh at the crisis of the Brisbane symphony no longer irritated Vashti; she accepted it as part of the melody. The jarring noise, whether in the head or in the wall, was no longer resented by her friend. And so with the mouldy artificial fruit, so with the bath water that began to stink, so with the defective rhymes that the poetry machine had taken to emit. All were bitterly complained of at first, and then acquiesced in and forgotten. Things went from bad to worse unchallenged.

It was otherwise with the failure of the sleeping apparatus. That was a more serious stoppage. There came a day when over the whole world—in Sumatra, in Wessex, in the innumerable cities of Courland and Brazil—the beds, when summoned by their tired owners, failed to appear. It may seem a ludicrous matter, but from it we may date the collapse of humanity. The Committee responsible for the failure was assailed by complaints, whom it referred, as usual, to the Committee of the Mending Apparatus, who in its turn assured them that their complaints would be forwarded to the Central Committee. But the discontent grew, for mankind was not yet sufficiently adaptable to do without sleeping.

"Someone is meddling with the Machine—" they began.

"Someone is trying to make himself king, to reintroduce the personal element."

"Punish that man with Homelessness."

"To the rescue! Avenge the Machine! Avenge the Machine!"

"War! Kill the man!"

But the Committee of the Mending Apparatus now came forward, and allayed the panic with well-chosen words. It confessed that the Mending Apparatus was itself in need of repair.

The effect of this frank confession was admirable.

"Of course," said a famous lecturer—he of the French Revolution, who gilded each new decay with splendour—"of course we shall not press our complaints now. The Mending Apparatus has treated us so well in the past that we all sympathize with it, and will wait patiently for its recovery. In its own good time it will resume its duties. Meanwhile let us do without our beds, our tabloids, our other little wants. Such, I feel sure, would be the wish of the Machine."

Thousands of miles away his audience applauded. The Machine still linked them. Under the seas, beneath the roots of the mountains, ran the wires through which they saw and heard, the enormous eyes and ears that were their heritage, and the hum of many workings clothed their thoughts in one garment of subserviency. Only the old and

M

the sick remained ungrateful, for it was rumoured that Euthanasia, too, was out of order, and that pain had reappeared among men.

It became difficult to read. A blight entered the atmosphere and dulled its luminosity. At times Vashti could scarcely see across her room. The air, too, was foul. Loud were the complaints, impotent the remedies, heroic the tone of the lecturer as he cried: "Courage! courage! What matter so long as the Machine goes on? To it the darkness and the light are one." And though things improved again after a time, the old brilliancy was never recaptured, and humanity never recovered from its entrance into twilight. There was an hysterical talk of "measures," of "provisional dictatorship," and the inhabitants of Sumatra were asked to familiarize themselves with the workings of the central power station, the said power station being situated in France. But for the most part panic reigned, and men spent their strength praying to their Books, tangible proofs of the Machine's omnipotence. There were gradations of terror—at times came rumours of hope—the Mending Apparatus was almost mended—the enemies of the Machine had been got under—new "nerve-centres" were evolving which would do the work even more magnificently than before. But there came a day when, without the slightest warning, without any previous hint of feebleness, the entire communication-system broke down, all over the world, and the world, as they understood it, ended.

Vashti was lecturing at the time and her earlier remarks had been punctuated with applause. As she proceeded the audience became silent, and at the conclusion there was no sound. Somewhat displeased, she called to a friend who was a specialist in sympathy. No sound: doubtless the friend was sleeping. And so with the next friend whom she tried to summon, and so with the next, until she remembered Kuno's cryptic remark, "The Machine stops."

The phrase still conveyed nothing. If Eternity was stopping it would of course be set going shortly.

For example there was still a little light and air—the atmosphere had improved a few hours previously. There was still the Book, and while there was the Book there was security.

Then she broke down, for with the cessation of activity came an unexpected terror—silence.

She had never known silence, and the coming of it nearly killed her—it did kill many thousands of people outright. Ever since her birth she had been surrounded by the steady hum. It was to the ear what artificial air was to the lungs, and agonizing pains shot across her head. And scarcely knowing what she did, she stumbled forward and pressed the unfamiliar button, the one that opened the door of her cell.

Now the door of the cell worked on a simple hinge of its own. It was not connected with the central power station, dying far away in France. It opened, rousing immoderate hopes in Vashti, for she thought that the Machine had been mended. It opened, and she saw the dim tunnel that curved far away towards freedom. One look, and then she shrank back. For the tunnel was full of people—she was almost the last in that city to have taken alarm.

People at any time repelled her, and these were nightmares from her worst dreams. People were crawling about, people were screaming, whimpering, gasping for breath, touching each other, vanishing in the dark, and ever and anon being pushed off the platform on to the live rail. Some were fighting round the electric bells, trying to summon trains which could not be summoned. Others were yelling for Euthanasia or for respirators, or blaspheming the Machine. Others stood at the doors of their cells fearing, like herself, either to stop in them or to leave them, and behind all the uproar was silence—the silence which is the voice of the earth and of the generations who have gone.

No—it was worse than solitude. She closed the door again and sat down to wait for the end. The disintegration went on, accompanied by horrible cracks and rumbling. The valves that restrained the Medical Apparatus must have been weakened, for it ruptured and hung hideously from the ceiling. The floor heaved and fell and flung her from her chair. A tube oozed towards her serpent fashion.

And at last the final horror approached—light began to ebb, and she knew that civilization's long day was closing.

She whirled round, praying to be saved from this, at any rate, kissing the Book, pressing button after button. The uproar outside was increasing, and even penetrated the wall. Slowly the brilliancy of her cell was dimmed, the reflections faded from her metal switches. Now she could not see the reading-stand, now not the Book, though she held it in her hand. Light followed the flight of sound, air was following light, and the original void returned to the cavern from which it had been so long excluded. Vashti continued to whirl, like the devotees of an earlier religion, screaming, praying, striking at the buttons with bleeding hands.

It was thus that she opened her prison and escaped—escaped in the spirit: at least so it seems to me, ere my meditation closes. That she escapes in the body—I cannot perceive that. She struck, by chance, the switch that released the door, and the rush of foul air on her skin, the loud throbbing whispers in her ears, told her that she was facing the tunnel again, and that tremendous platform on which she had seen men fighting. They were not fighting now. Only the whispers remained, and the little whimpering groans. They were dying by hundreds out in the dark.

She burst into tears.

Tears answered her.

They wept for humanity, those two, not for themselves. They could not bear that this should be the end. Ere silence was completed their hearts were opened, and they knew what had been important on the earth. Man, the flower of all flesh, the noblest of all creatures visible, man who had once made god in his image, and had mirrored his strength on the constellations, beautiful naked man was dying, strangled in the garments that he had woven. Century after century had he toiled, and here was his reward. Truly the garment had seemed heavenly at first, shot with the colours of culture, sewn with the threads of self-denial. And heavenly it had been so long as it was a garment and no more, so long as man could shed it at will and live by the essence that is his soul, and the essence, equally divine, that is his body. The sin against the body—it was for that they wept in chief; the centuries of wrong against the muscles and the nerves, and those five portals by which we can alone apprehend—glozing it over with talk of evolution, until the body was white pap, the home of ideas as colourless, last sloshy stirrings of a spirit that had grasped the stars.

"Where are you?" she sobbed.

His voice in the darkness said, "Here."

"Is there any hope, Kuno?"

"None for us."

"Where are you?"

She crawled towards him over the bodies of the dead. His blood spurted over her hands.

"Quicker," he gasped, "I am dying—but we touch, we talk, not through the Machine."

He kissed her.

"We have come back to our own. We die, but we have recaptured life, as it was in Wessex, when Aelfrid overthrew the Danes. We know what they know outside, they who dwelt in the cloud that is the colour of a pearl."

"But, Kuno, is it true? Are there still men on the surface of the earth? Is this—this tunnel, this poisoned darkness—really not the end?"

He replied:

"I have seen them, spoken to them, loved them. They are hiding in the mist and the ferns until our civilization stops. Today they are the Homeless—tomorrow—"

"Oh, tomorrow—some fool will start the Machine again, tomorrow."

"Never," said Kuno, "Never. Humanity has learnt its lesson."

As he spoke the whole city was broken like a honeycomb. An air-ship had sailed in through the vomitory into a ruined wharf. It crashed downwards, exploding as it went, rending gallery after gallery with its wings of steel. For a moment they saw the nations of the dead, and, before they joined them, scraps of the untainted sky.

The Aquatic Uncle

ITALO CALVINO

*The very first vertebrates to leave water and live on land
(many millions of years ago in the Coal Age) were descended
from a type of fish that had lungs, and fins that it could walk
on. The hero of this story, Qfwfq, has decided to "take the
plunge" and live on land, but as for his stubborn, old-fashioned
uncle . . .*

By then it was clear that the water period was coming to
an end,—*old Qfwfq recalled,*—those who decided to make
the great move were growing more and more numerous,
there wasn't a family that didn't have some loved one up
on dry land, and everybody told fabulous tales of the things
that could be done there, and they called back to their
relatives to join them. There was no holding the young fish;
they slapped their fins on the muddy banks to see if they
would work as paws, as the more talented ones had already
discovered. But just at that time the differences among us
were becoming accentuated: there might be a family that
had been living on land, say, for several generations, whose
young people acted in a way that wasn't even amphibious
but almost reptilian already; and there were others who
lingered, still living like fish, those who, in fact, became
even more fishy than they had been before.

Our family, I must say, including grandparents, was all
up on the shore, padding about as if we had never known
how to do anything else. If it hadn't been for the obstinacy
of our great-uncle N'ba N'ga, we would have long since
lost all contact with the aquatic world.

Yes, we had a great-uncle who was a fish, on my paternal
grandmother's side, to be precise, of the Coelacanthus
family of the Devonian period (the fresh-water branch:
who are, for that matter, cousins of the others—but I don't
want to go into all these questions of kinship, nobody can

ever follow them anyhow). So as I was saying, this great-uncle lived in certain muddy shallows, among the roots of some protoconifers, in that inlet of the lagoon where all our ancestors had been born. He never stirred from there: at any season of the year all we had to do was push ourselves over the softer layers of vegetation until we could feel ourselves sinking into the dampness, and there below, a few palms' lengths from the edge, we could see the column of little bubbles he sent up, breathing heavily the way old folk do, or the little cloud of mud scraped up by his sharp snout, always rummaging around, more out of habit than out of the need to hunt for anything.

"Uncle N'ba N'ga! We've come to pay you a visit! Were you expecting us?" we would shout, slapping our paws and tails in the water to attract his attention. "We've brought you some insects that grow where we live! Uncle N'ba N'ga! Have you ever seen such fat cockroaches? Taste one and see if you like it . . ."

"You can clean those revolting warts you've got with your stinking cockroaches!" Our great-uncle's answer was always some remark of this sort, or perhaps even ruder: this is how he welcomed us every time, but we paid no attention because we knew he would mellow after a little while, accept our presents gladly, and converse in politer tones.

"What do you mean, Uncle? Warts? When did you ever see any warts on us?"

This business about warts was a widespread prejudice among the old fish: a notion that, from living on dry land, we would develop warts all over our bodies, exuding liquid matter: this was true enough for the toads, but we had nothing in common with them; on the contrary, our skin, smooth and slippery, was such as no fish had ever had; and our great-uncle knew this perfectly well, but he still couldn't stop larding his talk with all the slanders and intolerance he had grown up in the midst of.

We went to visit our great-uncle once a year, the whole family together. It also gave us an opportunity to have a reunion, since we were scattered all over the continent; we

could exchange bits of news, trade edible insects, and
discuss old questions that were still unsettled.

Our great-uncle spoke his mind even on questions that
were removed from him by miles and miles of dry land,
such as the division of territory for dragonfly hunting; and
he would side with this one or that one, according to his
own reasoning, which was always aquatic. "But don't you
know that it's always better to hunt on the bottom and not
on the water's surface? So what are you getting all upset
over?"

"But, Uncle, you see: it isn't a question of hunting on
the bottom or on the surface. I live at the foot of a hill, and
he lives halfway up the slope . . . You know what I mean by
hill, Uncle . . ."

And he said: "You always find the best crayfish at the
foot of the cliffs." It just wasn't possible to make him
accept a reality different from his own.

And yet, his opinions continued to exert an authority
over all of us; in the end we asked his advice about matters
he didn't begin to understand, though we knew he could be
dead wrong. Perhaps his authority stemmed from the fact
that he was a leftover from the past, from his way of using
old figures of speech, like: "Lower your fins there,
youngster!" whose meaning we didn't grasp very clearly.

We had made various attempts to get him up on land
with us, and we went on making them; indeed, on this
score, the rivalry among the various branches of the family
never died out, because whoever managed to take our
great-uncle home with him would achieve a position of pre-
eminence over the rest of our relatives. But the rivalry was
pointless, because our uncle wouldn't dream of leaving the
lagoon.

"Uncle, if you only knew how sorry we feel leaving you
all alone, at your age, in the midst of all that dampness . . .
We've had a wonderful idea . . ." someone would begin.

"I was expecting the lot of you to catch on finally," the
old fish interrupted, "now you've got over the whim of
scraping around in that drought, so it's time you came
back to live like normal beings. Here there's plenty of
water for all, and when it comes to food, there's never been

a better season for worms. You can all dive right in, and we won't have to discuss it any further."

"No, no, Uncle N'ba N'ga, you've got it all wrong. We wanted to take you to live with us, in a lovely little meadow . . . You'll be nice and snug; we'll dig you a little damp hole. You'll be able to turn and toss in it, just like here. And you might even try taking a few steps around the place: you'll be very good at it, just wait and see. And besides, at your time of life, the climate on land is much more suitable. So come now, Uncle N'ba N'ga, don't wait to be coaxed. Won't you come home with us?"

"No!" was our great-uncle's sharp reply, and taking a nose dive into the water, he vanished from our sight.

"But why, Uncle? What have you got against the idea? We simply don't understand. Anyone as broad-minded as you ought to be above certain prejudices . . ."

From an angry huff of water at the surface, before the final plunge with a still-agile jerk of his tail fin, came our uncle's final answer: "He who has fleas in his scales swims with his belly in the mud!" which must have been an idiomatic expression (similar to our own, much more concise proverb: "If you itch, scratch"), with that term "mud" which he insisted on using where we would say "land".

That was about the time when I fell in love. Lll and I spent our days together, chasing each other; no one as quick as she had ever been seen before; in the ferns, which were as tall as trees in those days, she would climb to the top in one burst, and the tops would bend almost to the ground, then she would jump down and run off again; I, with slower and somewhat clumsier movements, followed her. We ventured into zones of the interior where no print had ever marked the dry and crusty terrain; at times I stopped, frightened at having come so far from the expanse of the lagoons. But nothing seemed so far from aquatic life as she, Lll, did: the deserts of sand and stones, the prairies, the thick forests, the rocky hillocks, the quartz mountains: this was her world, a world that seemed made especially to be scanned by her oblong eyes, to be trod by her darting steps. When you looked at her smooth skin, you felt that scales had never existed.

Her relatives made me a bit ill at ease; hers was one of those families who had become established on Earth in the earliest period and had finally become convinced they had never lived anywhere else, one of those families who, by now, even laid their eggs on dry terrain, protected by a hard shell, and Lll, if you looked at her when she jumped, at her flashing movements, you could tell she had been born the way she was now, from one of those eggs warmed by sand and sun, having completely skipped the swimming, wriggling phase of the tadpole, which was still obligatory in our less evolved families.

The time had come for Lll to meet my family: and since its oldest and most authoritative member was Great-Uncle N'ba N'ga, I couldn't avoid a visit to him, to introduce my fiancée. But every time an opportunity occurred, I postponed it, out of embarrassment; knowing the prejudices among which she had been brought up, I hadn't yet dared tell Lll that my great-uncle was a fish.

One day we had wandered off to one of those damp promontories that girdle the lagoon, where the ground is made not so much of sand as of tangled roots and rotting vegetation. And Lll came out with one of her usual dares, her challenges to feats: "Qfwfq, how long can you keep your balance? Let's see who can run closest to the edge here!" And she darted forward with her Earth-creature's leap, now slightly hesitant, however.   This time I not only felt I could follow her, but also that I could win, because my paws got a better grip on damp surfaces. "As close-to the edge as you like!" I cried. "And even beyond it!"

"Don't talk nonsense!" she said. "How can you run beyond the edge? It's all water there!"

Perhaps this was the opportune moment to bring up the subject of my great-uncle. "What of that?" I said to her. "There are those who run on this side of the edge, and those who run on the other."

"You're saying things that make no sense at all!"

"I'm saying that my great-uncle N'ba N'ga lives in the water the way we live on the land, and he's never come out of it!"

"Ha! I'd like to meet this N'ba N'ga of yours!"

She had no sooner finished saying this than the muddied surface of the lagoon gurgled with bubbles, moved in a little eddy, and allowed a nose, all covered with spiky scales, to appear.

"Well, here I am. What's the trouble?" Great-Uncle said, staring at Lll with eyes as round and inexpressive as stones, flapping the gills at either side of his enormous throat. Never before had my great-uncle seemed so different from the rest of us: a real monster.

"Uncle, if you don't mind ... this is ... I mean, I have the pleasure to present to you my future bride, Lll," and I pointed to my fiancée, who for some unknown reason had stood erect on her hind paws, in one of her most exotic poses, certainly the least likely to be appreciated by that boorish old relative.

"And so, young lady, you've come to wet your tail a bit, eh?" my great-uncle said: a remark that in his day no doubt had been considered courtly, but to us sounded downright indecent.

I looked at Lll, convinced I would see her turn and run off with a shocked twitter. But I hadn't considered how strong her training was, her habit of ignoring all vulgarity in the world around her. "Tell me something: those little plants there ..." she said, nonchalantly, pointing to some rushes growing tall in the midst of the lagoon, "where do they put down their roots?"

One of those questions you ask just to make conversation: as if she cared about those rushes! But it seemed Uncle had been waiting only for that moment to start explaining the why and the wherefore of the roots of floating trees and how you could swim among them and, indeed, how they were the very best places for hunting.

I thought he would never stop. I huffed impatiently, I tried to interrupt him. But what did that saucy Lll do? She encouraged him! "Oh, so you go hunting among those underwater roots? How interesting!"

I could have sunk into the ground from shame.

And he said: "I'm not fooling! The worms you find there! You can fill your belly, all right!" And without giving it a second thought, he dived. An agile dive such as I'd never seen him make before. Or rather, he made a leap into the air—his whole length out of the water, all dotted with scales—spreading the spiky fans of his fins; then, when he had completed a fine half-circle in the air, he plunged back, head-first, and disappeared quickly with a kind of screw-motion of his crescent-shaped tail.

At this sight, I recalled the little speech I had prepared hastily to apologize to Lll, taking advantage of my uncle's departure ("You really have to understand him, you know, this mania for living like a fish has finally even made him look like a fish"), but the words died in my throat. Not even I had ever realized the full extent of my grandmother's brother's fishiness. So I just said: "It's late, Lll, let's go..." and already my great-uncle was re-emerging, holding in his shark's lips a garland of worms and muddy seaweed.

It seemed too good to be true, when we finally took our leave; but as I trotted along silently behind Lll, I was thinking that now she would begin to make her comments, that the worst was still to come. But then Lll, without stopping, turned slightly toward me: "He's very nice, your uncle," and that was all she said. More than once in the past her irony had disarmed me; but the icy sensation that filled me at this remark was so awful that I would rather not have seen her any more than to have to face the subject again.

Instead, we went on seeing each other, going together, and the lagoon episode was never mentioned. I was still uneasy: it was no use my trying to persuade myself she had forgotten; every now and then I suspected she was remaining silent in order to embarrass me later in some spectacular way, in front of her family, or else—and, for me, this was an even worse hypothesis—she was making an effort to talk about other things only because she felt sorry for me. Then, out of a clear sky, one morning, she said curtly: "See here, aren't you going to take me to visit your uncle any more?"

In a faint voice I asked, "Are you joking?"

Not at all; she was in earnest, she couldn't wait to go back and have a little chat with old N'ba N'ga. I was all mixed up.

That time our visit to the lagoon lasted longer. We lay on a sloping bank, all three of us: my great-uncle was nearest the water, but the two of us were half in and half out, too, so anyone seeing us from the distance, all close together, wouldn't have known who was terrestrial and who was aquatic.

The fish started in with one of his usual tirades: the superiority of water respiration to air breathing, and all his repertory of denigration. "Now Lll will jump up and give him what for!" I thought. Instead, that day Lll was apparently using a different tactic: she argued seriously, defending our point of view, but as if she were also taking old N'ba N'ga's notions into consideration.

According to my great-uncle, the lands that had emerged were a limited phenomenon: they were going to disappear just as they had cropped up or, in any event, they would be subject to constant changes: volcanoes, glaciations, earthquakes, upheavals, changes of climate and of vegetation. And our life in the midst of all this would have to face constant transformations, in the course of which whole races would disappear, and the only survivors would be those who were prepared to change the bases of their existence so radically that the reasons why living was beautiful would be completely overwhelmed and forgotten.

This prospect was in absolute contradiction to the optimism in which we children of the coast had been brought up, and I opposed the idea with shocked protests. But for me the true, living confutation of those arguments was Lll: in her I saw the perfect, definitive form, born from the conquest of the land that had emerged; she was the sum of the new boundless possibilities that had opened. How could my great-uncle try to deny the incarnate reality of Lll? I was aflame with polemical passion, and I thought that my fiancée was being all too patient and too understanding with our opponent.

True, even for me—used as I was to hearing only grumblings and abuse from my great-uncle's mouth—this logically arranged argumentation of his came as a novelty, though it was still spiced with antiquated and bombastic expressions and was made comical by his peculiar accent. It was also amazing to hear him display a detailed familiarity—though entirely external—with the continental lands.

But Lll, with her questions, tried to make him talk as much as possible about life under water: and, to be sure, this was the theme that elicited the most tightly knit, even emotional discourse from my great-uncle. Compared to the uncertainties of earth and air, lagoons and seas and oceans represented a future with security. Down there, changes would be very few, space and provender were unlimited, the temperature would always be steady; in short, life would be maintained as it had gone on till then, in its achieved, perfect forms, without metamorphoses or additions with dubious outcome, and every individual would be able to develop his own nature, to arrive at the essence of himself and of all things. My great-uncle spoke of the aquatic future without embellishments or illusions, he didn't conceal the problems, even serious ones, that would arise (most worrying of all, the increase of saline content); but they were problems that wouldn't upset the values and the proportions in which he believed.

"But now we gallop over valleys and mountains, Uncle!" I cried, speaking for myself but especially for Lll, who remained silent.

"Go on with you, tadpole, when you're wet again, you'll be back home!" he apostrophized, to me, resuming the tone I had always heard him use with us.

"Don't you think, Uncle, that if we wanted to learn to breathe under water, it would be too late?" Lll asked earnestly, and I didn't know whether to feel flattered because she had called my old relative uncle or confused because certain questions (at least, so I was accustomed to think) shouldn't even be asked.

"If you're game, sweetie," the fish said, "I can teach you in a minute!"

Lll came out with an odd laugh, then finally began to run away, to run on and on beyond all pursuit.

I hunted for her across plains and hills, I reached the top of a basalt spur which dominated the surrounding landscape of deserts and forests surrounded by the waters. Lll was there. What she had wanted to tell me—I had understood her!—by listening to N'ba N'ga and then by fleeing and taking refuge up here was surely this: we had to live in our world thoroughly, as the old fish lived in his.

"I'll live here, the way Uncle does down there," I shouted, stammering a bit; then I corrected myself: "The two of us will live here, together!" because it was true that without her I didn't feel secure.

But what did Lll answer me then? I blush when I remember it even now, after all these geological eras. She answered: "Get along with you, tadpole; it takes more than that!" And I didn't know whether she was imitating my great-uncle, to mock him and me at once, or whether she had really assumed the old nut's attitude toward his nephew, and either hypothesis was equally discouraging, because both meant she considered me at a halfway stage, a creature not at home in the one world or in the other.

Had I lost her? Suspecting this, I hastened to woo her back. I took to performing all sorts of feats: hunting flying insects, leaping, digging underground dens, wrestling with the strongest of our group. I was proud of myself, but unfortunately whenever I did something brave, she wasn't there to see me: she kept disappearing, and no one knew where she had gone off to hide.

Finally I understood: she went to the lagoon, where my great-uncle was teaching her to swim under water. I saw them surface together: they were moving along at the same speed, like brother and sister.

"You know?" she said, gaily, "my paws work beautifully as fins!"

"Good for you! That's a big step forward," I couldn't help remarking, sarcastically.

It was a game, for her: I understood. But a game I didn't like. I had to recall her to reality, to the future that was awaiting her.

One day I waited for her in the midst of a wood of tall ferns which sloped to the water.

"Lll, I have to talk to you," I said as soon as I saw her, "you've been amusing yourself long enough. We have more important things ahead of us. I've discovered a passage in the mountains: beyond it stretches an immense stone plain, just abandoned by the water. We'll be the first to settle there, we'll populate unknown lands, you and I, and our children."

"The sea is immense," Lll said.

"Stop repeating that old fool's nonsense. The world belongs to those with legs, not to fish, and you know it."

"I know that he's somebody who is somebody," Lll said.

"And what about me?"

"There's nobody with legs who is like him."

"And your family?"

"We've quarreled. They don't understand anything."

"Why, you're crazy! Nobody can turn back!"

"I can."

"And what do you think you'll do, all alone with an old fish?"

"Marry him. Be a fish again with him. And bring still more fish into the world. Good-bye."

And with one of those rapid climbs of hers, the last, she reached the top of a fern frond, bent it toward the lagoon, and let go in a dive. She surfaced, but she wasn't alone: the sturdy, curved tail of Great-Uncle N'ba N'ga rose near hers and, together, they cleft the waters.

It was a hard blow for me. But, after all, what could I do about it? I went on my way, in the midst of the world's transformations, being transformed myself. Every now and then, among the many forms of living beings, I encountered one who "was somebody" more than I was: one who announced the future, the duck-billed platypus who nurses its young, just hatched from the egg; or I might encounter another who bore witness to a past beyond all return, a dinosaur who had survived into the beginning of the Cenozoic, or else—a crocodile—part of the past that had discovered a way to remain immobile through the centuries. They all had something, I know, that made them somehow superior to me, sublime, something that made me, compared to them, mediocre. And yet I wouldn't have traded places with any of them.